Wildwood Lodge

Wildwood Lodge

✳ *Snowfall Wishes* ✳

JENNIFER GRIFFITH

Wildwood Lodge

ASIN: B09JHQ82Z7
ISBN: 9798751988524

This is a work of fiction. Names, characters, places, and events are creations of the author's imagination or are used fictitiously. Any resemblance to actual persons, living or dead, events, or locations, is purely coincidental.

Cover art credit: Blue Water Books

For Everyone Who Dreams of a Perfect Christmas

Chapter 1

Jayne

Sounds of the WGWG newsroom pelted me but couldn't penetrate the rushing of adrenaline in my eardrums as I stared down at the text from my sister Joanie.

Sorry, Jayne. I think we'll skip it. Maybe next year. Merry Christmas!

"Oh, sweetie. You look like you just swallowed a bug in your eggnog." Gilda, my producer patted my shoulder—and then read over it. Her smile of mirth morphed to one of pity instantly. "Your sister? She's ditching you, too? Wasn't she the last of your siblings still coming? Oh, and you rented the Wilderness Lodge and everything."

Thanks for rubbing it in, boss. "Wildwood Lodge." But Gilda didn't know the half of it. With no siblings attending my holiday week, my career trajectory just took a nosedive, too. "I'll figure it out. Joanie might change her mind at the last minute. Jill, too." But not Jack or James. Okay, and not Joanie or Jill either.

Lame.

"At least there's this." Gilda placed a large, flat box on my desk. "Something from Albany Accents. They always send stuff your viewers go crazy for."

I shoved the Phone of Disappointment in my desk and used scissors to slice open the box. I pulled out the pink-and-red tinsel

1

wreath and held it up to glint in the light. "Wow! It's so pretty!"

Gilda stepped back. "I'm not sure about …"

A man halted near my cubicle, covering his eyes. "The camera will hate it. Hot video." He unshielded his eyes, and *oh, my stars.*

It was Ben Bellamy. My knees weakened at the demigod-like sight of the most popular small-market sportscaster in the whole country. He ruled all the ratings of this news station and kept the whole outfit in advertising dollars. *And he's at my desk.*

Criticizing my taste, but still.

Upon seeing our confused looks, he said, "Hot video? You know. When a color is too bright for the cameras and ends up over-modulated, with the color causing a bloom for the viewer?"

"I know hot video," I said—thinking of every clip I'd ever seen Ben star in.

"Well, that thing is more radioactive. If you feature that tacky thing, you'll give the viewers thyroid cancer."

Before I could argue with him that cancer jokes weren't all that funny, he sauntered off. The guy had a serious saunter on him. I might have watched every pace of it.

Gilda grabbed my sleeve and tugged hard. I peeled my gaze off the ghost of Ben Bellamy.

Gilda's eyes were bugging out. "You were just spoken to by Ben Bellamy."

"He told me I'd be giving my viewers a terminal illness."

"The *only* person Ben Bellamy ever talks to at this station is his producer, O'Keefe." Gilda fanned herself. "Did you catch his episode of 'Beyond the Bench' last night? Talk about hot video. His blue eyes were over-modulating the color feed."

Gilda was married with kids, but like every other woman I'd heard of in the past year, she was a devotee of the conundrum that was Ben Bellamy. And by conundrum, I mean how could he be so warm and friendly on camera and such a glacier in real life?

Well, he might be king of the sports world, but—"He knows

2

nothing about home decorating. And even less about my fan base."

"You might be right that your viewers will eat this thing up." Gilda picked it up. "Ouch. It's bristly."

Just like Ben Bellamy—who, at this moment, passed my desk again and deigned to comment. *Again.* "Genus: bristle brush; species: toilet. Don't put that on TV. Nothing about it says Christmas, Jayne."

He knew my name? My head swirled—like water going down a toilet, apparently, because I followed up with this retort, "Let me know if you want to use this brush for your too-white teeth, Sports Man." Sports Man. I could beat my head against the desk. "It's *cheery.* You wouldn't know cheer if it bit you in the leg."

Then, I was staring at his so-athletic legs again as he walked away.

"Whatever, Product Placement Jayne."

The second he was out of earshot, Gilda mouthed, *He knows your name!*

Oh, brother. It wasn't that big of a news station. "It's on the name of my show, 'Plain Jayne.'" And my show wasn't exactly *obscure.* No, I wasn't getting scouted relentlessly by Boston or New York City markets like Ben Bellamy, but I had a following of my own.

Which is why Marty and Marissa are coming to Wildwood Lodge in a pseudo-interview! There, they'd see whether my hostessing skills, my decorating, and my charm were a good fit for their Boston juggernaut show *Good Morning, USA.* Everyone in America watched it for the charm of the brother-sister duo.

Think of it! Me! On as Marty and Marissa's style person!

"And he gave you a nickname?" Her eyebrows waggled.

"Uh, point of fact, it's not all that nice of a nickname."

Well, one thing for sure, I had to make the Wildwood Lodge event work or I'd be out of more than just the reservation deposit. I'd also be missing my chance at showing Mom and Dad and my family that my job wasn't just a hobby. That my career wasn't a frivolous waste of time.

"Gilda, if you think this wreath won't work for the camera, maybe

3

I can use it for my Wildwood Lodge event instead."

"You're still doing it?"

"I mean, I paid the deposit." And I had two famous guests still on the roster.

"You know," Gilda said, leaning against my cubicle wall, "you could always invite other people."

"Like who? Christmas is about family." And yet, I had none, and I needed people to show up. But who else could I invite? Coworkers were out. Gilda, O'Keefe, Rita—*everyone* at WGWG had family or travel plans. My current roommates here in Albany had plans. My childhood friends Mallory and Emily had plans.

"Lots of people need a Christmas experience. Everybody does. If your family doesn't want to come, line up some strangers. Make them your family."

Without warning, the air around me tingled. Was she right? Could I do this for … strangers?

"Come on, Jayne. You write sales copy all the time. It's your whole morning spot, one ad after another. Just transfer those skills into an ad for the cabin."

The station boss hailed her, and Gilda jogged after him, leaving me and the too-bright wreath thinking together, sparkles of unexpected thoughts.

Frankly, people without family obligations at the holidays don't advertise it. There's a stigma. A swirl of pity—just like the one I'd seen on Gilda's face—hits when aloneness becomes apparent. I'd seen it too often: the *poor Jayne, she has no one* patronizing look that no one wants to encounter.

If I did this thing, and if I played it just right, I could help someone else avoid that piteous moment—and help myself defy the loneliness in the process.

This could work.

If the lodge owner didn't mind, maybe I could …

It all popped to life at once, like a heavenly vision, right down to a

4

subject line for the advertisement online: "Have Yourself a Perfect Little Christmas." With the word *yourself* in bold and all caps.

And then, the paragraph: "Join me for an all-Inclusive Christmas at the luxurious Wildwood Lodge in the breathtaking Adirondacks." It fleshed out quickly from there, hitting on all the activities and cheer I could provide.

Yes! I could just hear those sleigh bells jingling, ring-ting-tingling too. My fingers flew over the computer keys.

By the end of the afternoon, the ball wasn't just rolling, it was snowballing into an ideal avalanche of Christmas cheer—with the lodge owner's permission, three pages of scrawled notes, and five applicants for the experience already lining up.

Oh, yeah. I wasn't spending Christmas alone! And I was going to give someone—maybe several *someones*—their own, personalized holiday perfection.

Chapter 2

Ben

T he break area had just enough room for me and my disgust at Product Placement Jayne's ridiculousness. What on this green earth made her think a pink and red tinsel *anything* represented Christmas?

"And he shoots for two!" I aimed the orange Nerf foam ball at the basket attached to the break room door to throw away my show notes from last night. "And he—"

"Misses." Chief O'Keefe retrieved my ball from the counter near the coffee maker. "How you're so skilled at reporting on basketball, and every other sport, for that matter, and so *pathetic* at playing them, is a mystery."

"Remember, it's in your best interest to keep that secret locked down tight." I shot again and missed. It ricocheted and landed on my cheese Danish. Easy retrieval. "The viewers need to think I'm a former athlete."

"A video of your zero-point Nerf basketball score would go viral." O'Keefe poured himself a cup. "But, knowing you, it would only make your fans love you more."

"Love." I wiped the cream cheese off the ridges of the foam ball. "Pah."

"Luckily, they love you for your *mind*, not your body." He punched my shoulder.

I'd worked hard for that shoulder. "Hey." I rubbed it.

"It's even more important for that dark klutzy secret of yours to stay below the radar if you're going to go to New York City to report."

"I'm not doing that."

"Look, we all know you're talented enough. Frankly, we aren't even jealous—much—that you're getting scout emails weekly from bigger news outlets. Why not take one of them? This place isn't exactly …"

It was a dump, and we all knew it. But I loved it. "Maybe I like being a big fish in a small cesspool."

"Ha." O'Keefe wadded up his bagel wrapper and shot for two. He made it. "I'm serious, man."

"So am I." I gave the best nonchalant shrug I could muster. "There's stuff I still want to do in Albany."

"You've *conquered* Albany. And the replays of your show go viral online nationwide every night. Do you know, your biggest demographic is forty-five to seventy-five-year-old women?"

"Achievement unlocked." Little did he know, a seventy-five-year-old woman was the reason I couldn't leave town. Not that I'd tell O'Keefe about Grandma Bonnie or about her and Grandpa's untimely death.

I was one big task away from making restitution to them. But so far, I'd failed at the final piece of the puzzle for the past eight years since I finished my master's degree. It wasn't shaping up to be my year to fulfill it now, either.

"Fine. Have it your way. The rest of us don't mind sharing in your success as the top news market in Albany." He plopped down at the break room's only table. "You got your Christmas plans all set?"

7

It was small-talk, the kind everyone made, so it shouldn't have made my spine straighten. "Nah." The holidays did that to me, though. *Thanks to my big, last mission.* Guilt was blocking me, and I hated that it revolved around Christmas. But what could I do?

"Really? But I heard they're letting your underling have your spot for two weeks this holiday."

"He's eager." I shrugged and took a bite of the pastry. It tasted about as good as that toilet brush thing on Product Placement Jayne's desk a few minutes ago would have tasted. I pushed it away. "And he's the station manager's nephew, too."

"Ah." O'Keefe nodded knowingly and sipped his cup. "Not to harp, but why not take one of those metro-market jobs you keep getting scouted for? Make room for the kid?"

"Because I like living out here." Mostly. "Huge cities are frantic. In fact, I'd live further out if I could."

"What, in the forest?"

Actually, yeah. "Give me a remote house in the woods with no cell towers, no TV, no nothing. I'm so there."

Chief O'Keefe closed his eyes. "I could get into that. There's so much noise at Casa de O'Keefe we all need those hearing-protective earmuffs. They say silence is golden, but with four kids and five dogs, I get *no* trace of gold."

Rita, the lighting director, walked up. "House in the woods, huh?" Everyone in this newsroom was a chronic eavesdropper. "That'd be so great for Christmas. Cozy and quiet. I just saw an ad for one on social media, almost clicked on it." She whipped out her phone. "If I didn't have to slog my way over the river and through the cement jungle to Arlo's mother's house for overcooked turkey and fat-free mashed potatoes, I'd so be there." She swiped a couple of times and aimed her phone screen at me. "Check this out."

O'Keefe snared it first. "Have yourself a perfect little Christmas, huh?" He hummed and muttered the details. "Wildwood Lodge, Adirondacks, *multiple* fireplaces, wraparound deck, private bedroom with bathroom attached, all holiday amenities provided, including meals and Christmas cheer."

The air around me tingled.

He looked up at me. "You need this, dude."

"Ha," I offered, in an O'Keefeism. But the images blazed on the insides of my eyelids. Wraparound porch? Deck, mountains, silence and trees—nice, but not necessary. Perfect Christmas? Very promising.

No. I should ignore it. It was an advertisement, possibly a hoax. But those words, *perfect Christmas,* hooked me like they were dangled by Captain Ahab himself. "What exactly do they mean by Christmas cheer?" I snagged Rita's phone and read it for myself.

The ad promised everything holiday: food, music, decorating the tree, ice skating on a private pond.

The little voice whispered inside me—*this is your chance to make it right with Grandma.*

"Nope." I batted the voice and the temptation away out into the outfield. "Christmas with strangers? Isn't that the opposite of a perfect Christmas?"

Rita took her phone back with a shrug. "Not everyone has family. It's pretty hard to put yourself through all the paces of holiday-ifying your life if you're alone. Trust me, after my divorce I learned that one. Glad I remarried a guy with kids so that I could justify the effort again."

She and O'Keefe discussed the perils and stresses of family Christmases while I brain-surfed through the list of activities offered by the lodge host. Every one of them fit what I should have been trying to revive in my own life—since during my college years, I always made excuses, skipped some of Grandma's specially planned activities, took for granted what I had while I'd had it.

I'm sorry, Grandma.

For Grandma's sake, and to show her I'd learned since then, I'd do it. I'd experience and *appreciate* a perfect Christmas..

For Grandma's sake. A perfect Christmas. One worthy of Bonnie Bellamy. One worthy of filling in the final blank on my "make restitution to Grandma and Grandpa" card, after adjusting my course, keeping their Albany house and yard beautiful, and living the dream career Grandpa would have wanted. *Then I can leave Albany—without guilt or shame.*

"Did you see the hilarious coincidence?" Rita shoved the phone into her blazer pocket as she stood at the doorway to leave. "The host of that perfect Christmas thing's name? Jayne Renwick."

O'Keefe chortled. "It couldn't be. It's not the same woman."

"Not unless she has a secret life of wealth with a lavish forest-retreat home in the Adirondacks." Rita chortled back. "But if it *were* the same woman, and Bellamy here joined her little party, he could finally hit on her like we've all been plotting."

Plotting! "Trust me, Jayne Renwick is the *last* person on earth who could put on a perfect Christmas for me." That toilet brush thing? And all the other junk-level tackiness she showcased on her show? Never. Grandma would return from heaven and haunt me.

"What do you mean? She's gorgeous. Every guy in the station dreams of Jaynie with the light brown hair. And that smile?"

Her smile was actually quite fine. And her hair, I will admit, had something divine about it. Dancing with Jayne beside a dazzlingly lit Christmas tree to the strains of Bing Crosby's "White Christmas" did have its romantic appeal.

But the tastelessness of her taste obscured anything else that might be attractive about the woman. Jayne herself, a flibbertigibbet, was who came in the beautiful wrapping paper.

"Quit hesitating. Are you intimidated by her beauty or something? Because, dude, she's actually pretty nice and fun."

"No." Maybe a touch. Confidence always drew me to a woman, but her ineptitude might be contagious.

"Ben, trust me." Rita ate a carrot stick and talked through it. "Jayne's a perfectly great person. Do you even know her?"

"I've sat through meetings with her." Where she was frequently unprepared and flighty, two of my biggest pet peeves. "Stop plotting my dating life. I'll handle that when I'm ready." Once I'd handled everything necessary to make things right with my grandparents' memories, that was. "Plus, I'll bet you season tickets to the Buffalo Bills it's a different person."

I pulled out my phone to try background checking it, but I kept coming back to photos of Wildwood Lodge. That place was classic and classy—everything Jayne Renwick wasn't. It had to be a different person. The state of New York was huge. There were bound to be dozens of Jayne Renwicks.

"You're showing a lot of interest, Bellamy." Rita leaned against the doorframe, her eyebrows bouncing up and down like a New York Knicks ball in play. "Does that mean you're signing up for the house in the woods thing?"

"He has a couple weeks off." O'Keefe didn't keep secrets. "And nothing to do."

"Thanks, pal." I smirked at him.

"Is that right?" Rita nodded like she had my number.

So, what if she did? After five years of avoiding this last vestige of my penance, it was time. And at first glance at the house and the plans listed on the website, the opportunity seemed just right.

No, it seemed perfect.

Chapter 3

Jayne

A s I drove down the long, winding lane through the trees toward Wildwood Lodge, my breath caught. How could it have been more beautiful and cozy-looking in person than it had been in the online photo? I could have sworn the picture had been doctored, but no. It was real.

Snow piled all around it, with a glow in the windows, even at this time of day, made it seem like the most inviting place I'd ever seen.

I parked, and Gilda pulled up beside me. She'd come just to help drop things off.

"It's holiday magically delicious!" Gilda climbed out of her minivan and stretched her arms, hopping like a leprechaun. "Wonders can happen here."

I couldn't agree more. Something tingled inside me, as if something big was going to happen here at Wildwood Lodge for me.

Marty and Marissa, of course.

"Wow, it's a lot larger in person." Gilda threw her arms wide.

"I wasn't expecting it to be this grand." At all. The in-real-life vision enchanted me. Wildwood Lodge was so much more gorgeous, more cozy, than in photos. I could almost smell the wood-fire smoke coming from its chimney already, and we hadn't lit it yet.

Gilda and I began unloading the groceries from her van. She'd brought all the food, since my SUV was packed to the gills with Christmas cheer.

"Who all did you end up approving as your guests?" She re-hoisted the box of sugar cookie ingredients on her hip while I unlocked the cabin door. "Not that guy with the prison record, I hope."

I picked up the four gallons of milk and pushed the door open. "Oh, my lands. It's even bigger on the inside." And that was saying something.

We wandered in, our necks stretched back to stare at the log-trussed ceiling, the rock fireplace, the floor-to-ceiling windows opening onto the side deck with the Jacuzzi tub. It was grand and yet homey at the same time. Wood was stacked beside the fireplace, and practically every piece of furniture had soft cushions and chenille throw blankets draped across it.

I could have fallen into them and curled up for the winter.

"This is amazing. Kitchen, living room, all the books anyone could read in a lifetime. Where are the nine bedrooms?" Gilda asked, having apparently forgotten her prison-dude question. "Upstairs? Can I go look?"

We left our groceries on the granite-topped island of the chef's kitchen and took a gape-mouthed tour of Wildwood Lodge. Every bedroom was an opportunity for me to add little Christmasy details from the items I'd collected and brought.

Ooh! I could theme each bedroom!

"It's so rustic and so modern at the same time," Gilda said as we explored. "I keep thinking there will be animated teapots and singing feather dusters pop out at any moment telling us to be their guest." Gilda pushed open a bedroom door. "Are you going to choose a room first? You should take this one. Check out that view!"

Indeed, it had a dreamy view of the frozen pond, which had been one of the main reasons I'd selected one of the guests, the former figure skater.

"Oh, ice skating would be so romantic—with the right person." Gilda turned to me, pleading. "Please tell me at least *one* of your guests is going to be a potential love match for you. It's time, Jayne. You've accomplished so much in your career. You're established. It's a good season for love, don't you think?"

My face must have heated by a hundred degrees. "There might be someone. I'm—not sure, of course." And it might not be appropriate behavior for me to flirt with a guest in the first place, but he did *exactly* fit the description of someone I'd wished for ages ago—at a cabin pretty similar to Wildwood Lodge. "No, never mind."

Gilda's eyes flickered with interest. "Who? I saw the guest list."

"You peeked?"

"What kind of a friend—and producer—would I be if I let you go off to an isolated cabin in the woods with strangers whose background checks I hadn't run?"

"You're overprotective." I hugged her. "But also a good friend."

We went downstairs and kept unloading, traipsing through the snow to bring everything inside.

"Quit holding out on me, Jayne. Is the Mr. Possibility you have in mind the school teacher? The Army guy? Not the sports psychologist. I thought you were done with dating athletes."

"I am totally done with dating athletes." No one knew that better than Gilda. She'd been my shoulder to cry on too many times when I'd dated Paxton, José, Max, and Rhett. A few others, too, and with all of them the same demise—they'd shown interest long enough to get a good make-out from me, and then they'd literally instantly turned the TV back on and started watching the game.

It did something to a girl's self-image if she was less interesting than a ball—every time.

"Besides," I said, "sports psychologist isn't the same as an athlete. In fact, Benson Smith is probably a wannabe athlete. One of those jock-satellites. Those who can't do, analyze."

"Then, why approve his application to come to your perfect holiday?"

Good question. Out of dozens of applicants, his had stood out the most. It'd been the first one I'd chosen.

"His grandparents died a few years ago, and he doesn't have anyone else in his life. He said he misses his grandma, and that's why he applied."

"That's the only one I'm concerned about. There were red flags, Jayne. He was cagey about his profession on the paperwork, and then I couldn't find a single record about him. Not even a speeding ticket. Nobody is that squeaky clean. It's dangerous. I know it's last-minute, but I think you should contact him and cancel."

"You can't make me cancel Christmas for an orphan."

Gilda folded her arms over her chest. "If he's thirty-something, he's not an orphan. He's just a single guy."

Wrong. "If you've got no one, it doesn't matter how old you are." Maybe I was a metaphorical orphan.

"Fine. And I won't say *it's your funeral.*"

"Thank you."

"Even though I actually mean that in the literal sense." Gilda brought in the last of the groceries, and checked her watch. "Naya's recital is in three hours. Tell me quick if you're into the Army guy or the teacher so I don't die of curiosity on my snowy drive home. Speaking of funerals."

"I can't have you dying." She was my best friend these days, since Mallory and Emily had moved from Albany to Boston. "Okay, so, it's Calder Kimball. The history teacher."

Gilda made sparkle-fingers. "I saw his picture! He's one of those hot-nerd types." She gripped her hands together in excitement. "You going for the opposite of your usual type, then?"

Should I tell her? "Despite my athlete-dating history, the hot-nerd was my original *type*, if you want to know the truth." As briefly as possible, I gave her the low-down on my high school trip to a cabin similar to Wildwood Lodge.

And on my wish.

"You're saying that when you were sixteen, you and your friends believed that catching a snowflake from the first snowfall would let you wish on love?"

"Uh-huh."

"And that you've been holding out for that wish all these years?"

It'd been almost fifteen years, but, "Yeah. Why not?"

"You'd better tell me about that wish of yours." Gilda descended the steps. "So I'll have someone to dream about when I'm driving back."

"You're married."

"I'm a daydreamer." Gilda led me to her car, where she refused to get in until I told her every detail.

I described Mr. Deloitte. "The guy was every girl in the school's daydream. Piercing blue eyes, philosophical, a deep thinker. Fair hair, cut close." We'd watched him in class instead of the literary movies he'd shown us.

Gilda chuckled. "You do know that your insanely hot coworker looks just like the English teacher you just described, right? Blond locks, the sultriest eyes, and the perfect jaw-line. Women from sixteen to sixty-and-up leave comments on his streaming channel about how dreamy he is."

"Not *exactly* like him. Ben Bellamy is brawnier than Mr. Deloitte was." His shoulders could've eclipsed Mr. Deloitte. Hey, but we weren't talking about Ben Bellamy. "I'm not saying that Mr. Kimball is going to be anything like Mr. Deloitte. I'm just saying that when a single-guy history teacher applied, I recalled my girlhood wish, and I wasn't going to let the chance slip past me."

"Good for you." Gilda hugged me tightly. "When Mr. Kimball turns out to be Mr. Dreamboat, you have to text me and tell me, okay?"

She drove away, and I started moving all the activity-supplies and decorating boxes inside. Wow, there was no way I'd be able to fill up this space with the stuff I'd brought. Not a chance.

I went in the bathroom and hung up some of the holiday curtains I'd brought, and set out some of the other décor from my work stash and my personal stash.

This would never cover it all.

Think, think, think. There had to be a solution.

Oh, look! There was a piano! I dropped my box and went over to play for a bit. "Sleigh Ride" was my best piece. I got to the end, and the solution hit me. I whipped out my phone.

Hi. If you have something special that "means Christmas to you" that you'd like to bring to share with the other guests, please bring it. No matter how big or small, your holiday magic is welcome at Wildwood Lodge.

If everyone brought a little something, then they might not notice how little I'd brought along.

It was time I got started on the big room and the porch. From the first tote, I pulled out the wreath from last month's Albany Accents offering—the triple-layer pink, red, and white one. The bane of Ben Bellamy's existence was perfect for the front door of the lodge. It would beam a beacon of welcome and cheer, visible from the turnoff at the main road a mile away. How was that for radioactivity being put to good use?

I patted it, fluffing some of the pink tinsel. It looked nothing like a toilet brush now, in its intended natural environment.

Behind me, gravel crunched and an engine sounded. Someone pulled into the driveway in a huge pickup truck, the back of which was covered with a tarp, but I could see some telltale signs of holiday décor poking out. A tall guy wearing a knitted beanie cap and sunglasses jumped out of the driver's seat. He strode with sexy confidence and detached one corner of his tarp. Underneath, I spotted lighted reindeer—the classy kind,—a beautiful roof-gable angel in a soft blue dress with banners streaming from her hands, and a box the size of my sofa labeled *lights*.

Donner and Blitzen! It was a holiday miracle.

Honestly, he was kind of my own version of a fantasy Santa Claus, driving up in a new pickup instead of a fancy sleigh, and looking like he'd stepped off the pages of a fashion magazine, and …

Oh, my gosh. He pulled off his sunglasses.

No. It couldn't be. The burly version of Mr. Deloitte was unmistakable. But—

"Ben Bellamy?" The king of WGWG couldn't be here. Not in my wildest dreams. Or nightmares. "What in the North Pole are you doing at Wildwood Lodge?"

I didn't need to ask. He and his judgmental attitude were here *to ruin my perfect Christmas!*

Chapter 4

Ben

When I drove up to the Wildwood Lodge, I got two shocks. First, the shock of how incredible the setting was—like something out of a perfect painting by Currier and Ives from a century ago. Snow-covered beauty. Isolated cabin perfection. I expected a horse-drawn sleigh to pass at any moment. The cabin sat in the clearing near a thick stand of woods, at the edge of a smooth, snow-covered pond.

Tingles flew from my scalp, down my neck, and out my fingertips.

Something big was going to happen here. *I'll finally have a perfect Christmas—just the kind Grandma had planned for the year she died.*

Or it might be something more.

Then, however, I got my second shock—this one less magical—when I recognized who stood on the porch of Wildwood Lodge.

To be clear, only a few times in my life have I thought my head would spin around like a character's in a cartoon and twist-pop off.

This was one of them.

"Product Placement Jayne? *You're* the Jayne Renwick from the ad?" Which meant—I owed someone season tickets to the Buffalo Bills now. Curses danced on the tip of my tongue.

Jayne looked as taken aback as I felt—but much prettier. She wore a soft-looking blue sweater that set off her skin and eyes much better than anything wardrobe put her in at the station. Plus, she was lovely against a woodsy, wintry background. Her hair ruffled in the pine-scented breeze.

If I didn't already know what a disaster she was, I might have looked longer.

But as it was, I didn't need to. If she of the gaudy Christmas taste was the one running this event, I was out of here.

"Are you here to … sabotage me?"

Sabotage! "What could possibly motivate me to do that?" I shoved the box with Grandma's special angel back under the tarp. *Load it up and move it out.*

"I have a short guest list. Are you"—there came some spluttering—"friends with Chieko Parsons?"

"Who's Chieko Parsons?" Sounded like the same name as an ice skating champ whose story I'd covered during the Olympics back in college. "I mean … yes and no. If it's the same person I met a long time ago."

"She's a guest." Jayne marched down the porch steps to the open back door of an SUV stacked with boxes. "Unlike you."

"Well, I signed up for the *Have Yourself a Perfect Christmas* experience that apparently *you* advertised." As if *Jayne Renwick* and *perfect* could be used in the same sentence. "But it was clearly a mistake on my part."

Much as it would disappoint Grandma, this was obviously not the right venue for me to resurrect the Christmas spirit in my life.

Not with Product Placement Jayne and her army of tacky ideas at the helm.

"I do not have a Ben Bellamy on the list." She pulled a box—from the bottom of a stack—out of her truck, toppling the three that had been above it. "Believe me, I would have noted a Ben Bellamy."

And not approved him? Was that the implication? "Is Benson Smith on the list?" I stuck out a hand as if we were first meeting and not colleagues at WGWG. Make that, competitors—for the most advertising dollars. "It's my legal name, listed on my driver's license and on all my credit cards." I really should get around to making Bellamy my official last name—and booting the final vestiges of my deadbeat dad from my life.

"No guests are expected until after seven tonight." Jayne accepted the handshake, but she eyed me like I was the punt blocker and she was ready to kick the football. "Are you infiltrating, spying on me for the boss, or trying to ruin my holidays?"

"I'm …" My eye fell on the toilet brush of a wreath pinned to the front door. Gross. But then I gazed up at the biggest luxury home in the woods I'd ever seen. It was like it had materialized out of a Bing Crosby and Danny Kaye movie, a true Holiday Inn.

Grandma would have gone into palpitations of joy over it.

And this woman had defiled it with her plastic junk.

Tragic.

Product Placement Jayne was gorgeous, no question. And the way she wore that cashmere sweater, its contours hugging hers, I was drawn to her, undeniably and irresistibly—but only with my physical self.

My logical self, meanwhile, hollered for me to put down my ticket and step away from the crazy train.

"I showed up early, thinking I shouldn't miss any of the decorating, in case you started prior to guest check-in time. You said you wanted help." I held up my phone screen, waving her own text at her. "You did say to bring things."

To be honest, I'd loaded my truck with Grandma's precious things long before the text arrived. In fact, I was on the final curves before the cabin when her text chimed. I'd wanted to bring Grandma along. I'd figured I'd ask permission when I arrived, but the permission came to me along the way.

Jayne mashed her full lips together as if suppressing a mean

21

comment. It didn't change how pretty she looked. In fact, her brown eyes were even brighter with that emotion lighting them.

"Look, if you want me to, I'll leave."

"That's entirely up to you."

"I mean … I'd at least like to look around the house first." *For Grandma's sake.* I could almost hear her voice from Beyond chewing me out for skipping the chance to gather all the information before making my decision.

Grandma had often reminded me that I tended to skip perfectly good chances.

"The preparations aren't finished yet. The decorating, I mean. I have a ton of things to do still, but the grand piano distracted me."

"I'm sorry?" What did she mean by that? Don't tell me Product Placement Jayne played piano well enough to dare touch a grand piano. That'd be like hockey star Dempsey Dean Davidson revealing his secret hobby of needlepoint. "You play piano?"

"Of course. Everyone in my family does. Renwick requirement."

Jayne didn't demonstrate. Instead, she headed toward the door with her tote labeled *Personalized Sweaters and Mugs.* Just great. Classic Product Placement Jayne.

"Were these donated by your show's sponsors?" I hauled a different tote, labeled *Seasonal Pajama Gifts* and followed.

On the porch steps, she whipped around and seared me with her stare. "Don't let me keep you, since you obviously view me as someone incapable of creating Christmas cheer. Scoot along, Sports Brain."

Sports Brain! "Is that what you call me behind my back?"

"Among other things."

Usually, women said different things behind my back and in the comment sections of my streaming videos and news articles. Things about wanting to date me. And more. I guess I'd gotten used to the more-flattering words. Jayne certainly wasn't like the thousand eyelash-fluttering women throwing themselves at me any time I went to the grocery store.

One had even accosted me in the parking lot, offering to bear my children. Okay, that had happened three times.

No, I hadn't accepted.

"You can look around." Jayne held the door open for me, almost impatiently.

Inside, it took a moment for my eyes to adjust and take in the vaulted interior.

"You said it's not finished." There wasn't a single note of Christmas music or whiff of baking gingerbread in the air. Not a pine bough or bow to be seen. "Correct me if I'm wrong, but it looks like you haven't started."

"Of course I have." She set down her box and indicated a jumbled pile of other boxes, none of which were open. "I hung up the shower curtains."

"There weren't shower curtains in place at a luxury lodge? You had to bring your own?"

"There weren't any *holiday* shower curtains. Or bath mats or matching toilet sets."

"Toilet sets!" I bit back a few choice comments. I dropped my armload on a leather nail-head sofa. "You're kidding."

"Of course I'm not kidding." She headed back outside to the tumbling-out pile of boxes at her vehicle. "Apparently you want nothing to do with it, though. Maybe you should get on your way. But there are no refunds based on preferences against cute *Santa in a towel* shower curtains."

No refunds for a horror show when you expect a Hallmark movie? "Have you ever heard the term false advertising?" I grabbed another box and followed her inside again.

"Yes, I have. And it applies to Ben Bellamy, who advertised himself as Benson Smith, thank you very much."

That was a fair point, considering the circumstances. Jayne had called herself Jayne Renwick, no hidden identities.

"The lodge is beautiful." I attempt a truce. "Do you know its history?"

"Some of the documentation claims it was built by the Vanderbilts during the Great Camp era."

"Where rich New Yorkers left the city to supposedly *rough it* upstate, but all the while they brought servants and every modern convenience to the mountains with them?"

"Impressive."

"What, that I know a little about New York history and I'm not just a Sports Brain?"

"Look, Ben. Benson. Ben. Whatever." She set down her fuchsia-colored tote box. "I promised guests an experience. No, it's not department-store worthy right now. Why? Because I believe all that—decorating the tree and the home, choosing the music, baking the meals, frosting the cookies, making the gingerbread house—should be done together. It's not just presented on a platter. Where's the joy in that? The joy is in the messiness."

Whoa. Just a moment there. "I was with you up to joy. But messiness?" Messiness was chaos, not joy. "I'll help you finish unloading." But then I was out of here. "I didn't sign up for messiness." Christmas was pristine snowfields, perfectly tuned orchestral music, every light on the tree strung just right, and so on—and no mess.

Jayne, for all her pretty brown eyes and soft blue sweater contours, was the epitome of messiness.

Nope.

"Look, Ben. You're a celebrity. I know that. You're used to having things your way."

"Hey." I wasn't a celebrity. I worked at the same news station as Jayne did. She had a half-hour show, and I only had ten minutes, tops. "I'm not like that."

"Recent events and comments indicate otherwise. So, you can ditch this joint based on how wrong you think I am. I won't cry. But you should know there are several other people coming who will completely disagree with you. If you stay, I'll prove it to you. They

24

want to *experience* Christmas, not just view it through glass or on TV or whatever. They're tired of sitting on the sidelines. They want to be part of the action. It's why they signed up."

Good for them, if they chose chaos. But … okay. I was melting under the heat of her glare.

Jayne stood in front of me, planting her hands on her hips. "Why did you sign up, Ben? So you could come and criticize me? Because that's what my gut shouted the second I recognized you outside in your GQ stance."

She thinks I look like a magazine model? "No." Not at all.

"Or was it like you said on your application?"

My memory stretched back. What had I divulged to this woman that I never would have mentioned if I'd realized she was *the* Jayne Renwick? "What do you mean?"

"You told me you're without parents or grandparents. Without cousins or aunts or uncles. Without siblings. That your grandma loved Christmas. That you owe it to her to try to experience it."

"I wrote all that?" My neck heated up. Good thing I wore a scarf to obscure any telltale redness.

"I didn't select *you* from two hundred applications because you're Ben Bellamy, famous sports reporter. I chose you because your application whispered that you have a heart."

If so, it was lodged right up in the center of my throat.

I cleared it. "Well, you're the first to make that fatal error."

I should've left. I should've just walked away from the whole thing. It was already an exercise in humiliation and disappointment beyond anything I could've dreamed.

"I don't think so, Ben." Her eyes were soft, irresistible, healing.

"Then, I guess you're wrong. I'll just see you at the station. Good luck." I headed back out to my truck, buttoning down the edge of the tarp I'd prematurely unhooked.

"Wait a second." She was at my side, peeling at the tarp. "What's under here?"

I closed my eyes and rubbed a hand over my neck. "Nothing. Another mistake."

She pushed her way past me, lifting the edges of the tarp all around. "It's not nothing." Her head whipped around and her eyes were afire. "How did you know to bring this? Because I didn't send the text until half an hour ago. It's a two-hour drive."

"Yeah, okay. I just thought …"

"Thought what?" She stepped closer, and the breeze caught something peppermint on her skin, wafting it toward me. "Are you a mind-reader? Did you have a gut feeling I would fatally underestimate the size of the house here and misjudge how many acre-feet of Christmas decorations I'd need? That I'd be last-minute drowning?"

"You didn't even measure?"

She looked at her toes.

Of *course* she hadn't measured. Or planned. She'd showed up here with no idea how she would accomplish what she'd promised people she'd deliver. But she was being vulnerable and I couldn't attack her more. "Not a mind-reader, no. But it seems like you could have asked for the dimensions."

"I didn't think I'd need them. It looked similar to a place I'd been to before, a long time ago. I had … expectations."

Assumptions, she meant. "So your family did holidays up the mountains all together, huh?" Now I was prying into her past. "Lots of good memories? Piano music and Renwick family kitsch enough to choke a horse?" They probably had an aluminum tree and listened to that horrible Christmas album with all the synthesizers.

Her face went blank. "We … didn't celebrate Christmas as a family."

All the breath went out of my lungs. Probably the altitude. That had to be it. "I … oh. Okay." Now I sounded like an idiot. An insensitive one. Grandma Bonnie's stink-eye penetrated the veil of death and singed me. "Not even singing, or presents, or a tree?"

She shook her head. "I thought one year they'd get me a musical jewelry box. I'd asked for it, but instead, they gave me plane tickets. We went to Nicaragua."

Nicaragua. That didn't sound festive. "Well, Wildwood Lodge would have been a nice place for it, if you had."

Cringe. I was a cringe incarnate.

"I had a week with friends at the holidays once." She frowned. "They told their parents that I'd never had a proper Christmas, and they all were allowed to come up for the week between holidays, so I got a taste of it. Since then, I've always craved a repeat."

Her family didn't give her Christmas? And Jayne—being far more fancy than plain—was just the type who'd thrive in the bustle and festive hoopla. She'd had to beg friends to give it to her, and there'd never been a repeat.

A pine-scented breeze touched my skin and flapped the edge of the tarp. "I take it you're an only child like me?" Ninety percent of me wanted to leave, but here I stood asking questions.

"Nope. Youngest of five."

"But still no Christmas?"

My reporter-mind would have to dig into why later, but Product Placement Jayne needed this holiday experience on a deep level.

Just like I did.

Which meant the last thing I could do was leave—even though this disaster was one of her own creation. Under those revelations, how could I possibly leave? I couldn't haul my decorations away when she obviously needed them. I was painting my own character worse and worse.

I went up onto the porch. Jayne followed.

"You honestly don't have enough supplies to make the event happen?" I peeked inside one of the many boxes on the wraparound porch. Oh, no. No, no, no. "Because these don't count."

"What do you mean, they don't count? And I have supplies—cookie cutters, Christmas crossword puzzles, board games, craft-making materials. Just not enough garlands. Please. And"—I repeated—"what do you mean, they don't count?"

"There are flamingos in here. And trolls. And huge red and green plastic—what are those?"

"Poinsettias. To plant out front."

I pulled one out, pinching it with my thumb and index finger, holding it at arm's length. *She is planting plastic flowers.* Oh, merciful Grandma, let me leave?

"Hey. Those are mine." She snatched them back. "I've been collecting them to support vendors I've featured on Plain Jayne for the past few years. They're my personal belongings."

"I'm calling a personal foul on them."

"Why do you care? You're not even staying."

Much as I did not want to be part of red-and-green plastic anything, I couldn't let her flail. Not when she'd chosen my profile of all the people who'd applied. And especially not considering what I now knew about her—and what my grandparents would think of me if I left her high and dry.

"Fine, Jayne. You're welcome to anything I brought with me." Huge sigh of resignation. "What do you have planned, exactly?"

"Really?" Her eyes lit up, which made me feel suddenly like a quarterback whose twenty-yard pass connected. "I researched each guest's favorite movie, and we're watching one each night. I have them right … somewhere." She looked around helplessly.

Movies. She'd planned movies. If that was the extent of her planning, heaven help us. "What about activities, meals, entertainment, and so on?"

"I'm still working on the rest."

Guests would arrive at seven. *Tonight.* "Yes, I'll let you use my stuff, and I'll stay—but on one very firm condition."

"Name it." She clasped her hands. She was in a lot of hot water right now.

I was mentally rubbing my hands together at my potential victory here. "I will be the one to define *perfect* when it comes to the perfect

Christmas." A warm feeling rushed through me. Maybe it was Grandma's approval.

Giving a perfect Christmas might be more important than experiencing one. And no one needed a real Christmas more than this forlorn but feisty creature in front of me.

Jayne definitely needed me. *Why did that thought seem like the source of the warm feeling?*

Chapter 5

Jayne

"All right," I said, as we went back inside where it was warm. "You can have your condition."

Ben stared at me like I had grown a jingle bell on the end of my nose. "You're not going to fight me on my condition?"

"Why should I? I love Christmas, but I don't have a lot of preconceived notions about how it should be." None, in fact. "My only request is that when the other guests come, we quiz them about what would define a perfect Christmas for each of them, and we cater to that—make something happen for each person."

His jaw dropped and he held up a finger as if to say *just a minute there*. But soon, his hand fell, and his mouth relaxed. It was a very good mouth. The way his lips had that fullness, like he'd plumped them at a collagen spa or whatever. I could see why the comments below his videos were half gushing about his insightful commentary into the human soul, and the other half gushing about his dreamy good looks. I was getting a little dreamy-eyed myself. Again. Ben Bellamy was right here with me, looking as good as a ripe peach on a hot summer's day.

30

"Jayne?" Ben tapped my arm. "Jayne?"

Oh, great. I'd glazed over in peach thoughts.

"I asked who all is coming." Ben helped me, and we began to spread out decorations from the boxes he'd brought.

"I'd tell you about them, but why don't we make a game of it? You like games."

"I like sporting events, not games," Ben said.

"Potato, potahto. It's a guessing game. It'll give you a chance to look smart."

"Because I'm a Sports Brain?" He was avoiding placing the decorations I'd already lugged inside—probably thinking he'd contract a disease from them, such as a soft spot for what he called tackiness.

"Exactly." I didn't actually think he was dumb—at all. Talking to Ben Bellamy, sports king, just brought out some kind of unexpected contrariness in me. I couldn't help myself. "You saw my stack of movies. I'll tell you about the person, and you guess which one from the stack is their favorite movie."

"You think you can infer something about a person by their favorite movie, and vice versa?"

"I think you can tell a lot. Come on, you're the psychology fanatic. Impress me."

"Fine. Batter up." He set down the box he'd been carrying, and we unloaded a trio of glass angels. "Who's first?"

I ran through the guests, from Lester the Army vet, to Chieko the ice skating pianist, to Seneca the divorced nurse, to Calder the teacher, to Marty and Marissa—although I didn't use their names, and I wasn't a hundred percent sure when they'd show up or how long they'd stay. An hour? The whole week?

I laid out the movies. "Match them up."

"I'm guessing *It's a Wonderful Life* for the nurse."

"Nope. *Die Hard.*"

"You're joshing me."

"See? You can tell something about people—that they're

31

unexpected."

We went through, and he guessed almost all of them wrong. "At least I got my own right. 'White Christmas.'"

"Points for you." I offered him a high five, and then awkwardly changed to a fist-bump, and then back again, and our palms connected—*slowly*.

Heat radiated from his palm into mine, warming my arm and shoulder. I stared into his eyes, and something was there.

I pulled my hand away and pushed back whatever I'd seen in his gaze. Way back.

I mean, I had Calder Kimball coming, my wished-for teacher. A gift from the first-snowfall wish. I couldn't mess that up.

We continued putting out the decorations throughout the afternoon, but we didn't talk anymore. I kept glancing at Ben, and he was studiously avoiding looking at me, and even went outside to string lights and climb up to the roof's peak and place a pretty angel he'd brought.

He felt something too. I know he did. This was not what I wanted. At all. I mean, yeah—who wouldn't want the brilliant and gorgeous and famous Ben Bellamy? But still. Other plans.

A knock came at the front door. My chest lurched. "Is it seven already?" I hadn't even started making dinner! The lodge looked better—although we had no tree—but there was nothing to feed the guests as of yet.

"Not yet." Ben checked his phone. "Someone's early, like me. Want me to get the door?"

We went together, and there stood a burly, muscular guy covered with tattoos, beside a tiny ballerina-like Japanese girl.

"You must be Chieko." I reached for her, giving her a hug. "I'm Jayne. Welcome to Wildwood Lodge."

Ben greeted the tattooed guy, who must be Lester. They shook hands and brought in the luggage, taking it toward the rooms.

Chieko came inside, sending a look at Ben. "Is that your husband?

32

I've seen him somewhere. He looks so familiar."

"We're not married. He's a guest who arrived early." Everyone knew Ben—my suspicion was confirmed yet again. "If he looks familiar it may be because he's on TV. Sports guy on WGWG, *Beyond the Bench with Ben Bellamy*."

"Ben Bellamy! Right!" She grinned, showing a set of cute, white teeth. "I didn't know he'd landed a TV deal. He should. I bet women everywhere tune in for any show he's on."

They did. "If not from TV, how do you know him?"

"Chieko Parsons?" Ben walked over and took her by both hands. "Imagine running into you again after all these years." They caught up, and I—of course—eavesdropped. It turned out one of Ben's first sports news stories had been covering Chieko's meteoric rise in the ice skating world. "What are you doing here for Christmas? I thought you have family. I remember your father was your manager."

"They're on the West Coast now, relocated for Mom's work. I couldn't get a flight this time of year. I'm teaching piano, and that's not the way to wealth, in case you're wondering. But I love it." She turned to me. "I guess you already know Lester. He and I met outside."

Lester came down the stairs and picked up a bright purple suitcase from the pile of luggage. *See what I mean about expectations?* But then, he set it near Chieko.

"If you need help carrying it up to your room, let me know." Little love-hearts practically floated from his eyes at her. "I can carry it. Or anything else."

Chieko's gaze darted to his muscular biceps, which were bulging even through his flannel shirt. "Thanks, Lester." Her pupils dilated, I could've sworn it. And their gazes lingered on each other.

"You guys get settled in your rooms," I said. "I'll get dinner started."

Ben followed me into the kitchen, maybe not wanting to be a third wheel. "What meal do you have planned for tonight?"

"Planned?" I hadn't planned, not exactly. I'd brought ingredients for five days' worth of meals, but I hadn't outlined which would happen when.

Ben looked at me as if I'd just told him I didn't like the New England Patriots. "Not even for the first night?"

"I mean, there's spaghetti."

"For a holiday meal? You're kidding."

I wasn't. Why would I be? "I never kid about pasta. It is sacred."

The doorbell rang. I went to get it, while Ben filled a pot with water.

"You must be Seneca." I hugged her. "Welcome to Wildwood Lodge."

"It's just as snowy as in the picture." The nurse looked just like her pictures. She entered the room, gazing at the rafters, her jaw dropping. "It's huge. I love it. When do we eat? I'm starved."

"Soon." Yikes. I'd better get on that. "Are you a fan of pasta?"

"Who isn't? But I'm a bit of a stickler about it. Would you mind—terribly—if I did the cooking tonight?"

I stopped in my tracks. "Excuse me?"

"Or even for the week?" Seneca patted her cheeks. "I know, I know. You probably have everything all outlined. Maybe I could just be your *sous* chef." She bit her lower lip. "Of course, I'm a bit of a pain when I can't be the one in charge, so maybe I should just stay out of the kitchen altogether so as not to step on your toes, even though it's really my happy place, and if I can't cook, it won't feel like the holidays to me."

"Please, Seneca. You would not be stepping on my toes, but I'd hate to saddle you with that work."

"Work! It's not work. It's a joy to create food."

"Then, by all means!" I stepped back and waved my arm like I was a game-show hostess. "The kitchen is this way, and I'm happy to give you full charge of it. Let's go show you every crevice."

"You mean that?"

I meant every word. "Unless Ben here wants to fight you for it."

34

We walked in to find Ben Bellamy wearing a chef's apron and measuring salt into a steaming pot of water. "Ben, this is Seneca. She *loves* to cook, and it won't feel like Christmas to her if she can't do the cooking."

"I cook best for a crowd." She bustled in, almost bumping him aside. "You don't mind, do you? Wow, you're cute. Where have I seen you before?"

"Seneca, this is Ben Bellamy."

"From TV?" Stars lit her eyes. Ugh. But who was I to judge? I'd practically had the full zodiac of constellations in my eyes every time he'd spoken up in staff meeting for the past year and when I'd watched and rewatched his shows on a loop over the weekends. "I'm so pleased to meet you. If you want to share my kitchen, you can anytime." Except her tone implied a different room in the house instead of the kitchen.

"Don't let me intrude." He took off his apron and placed it over her shoulders. She turned around, and he tied it behind her waist. "I'm at your service, though, if you need a helper."

"Much as that offer is the most tempting thing to me since Nestlé invented milk chocolate, I really am a beast at the stove and do much better on my own. I'll make a more favorable impression on you if we don't work together on meals."

"Have at it, Seneca." He gave me a look that said *You are the luckiest person ever.* "Trust me, you won't be getting into Jayne's way—not a bit."

"You don't cook, Jayne?" She nosed through cupboards and opened the fridge.

I cooked. Ramen. Other boxed dinners. "It's fine, Seneca. I love that this will match your idea of a perfect Christmas. I'll do anything you need, and if you want me to head to town for additional ingredients, let me know."

"This place is amazingly well stocked. Did you bring all this food and these spices?"

I sure had. And I let Ben know it with a smug cock of the head.

"See?" I whispered. "I'm not the *worst* planner."

"Is everyone here already?" Seneca asked.

"We still lack a few. One is a history teacher, and the other two—" The doorbell rang, cutting off my confusion about whether or not to mention Marty and Marissa yet.

Ben and I headed to answer it together—even though I knew who it would probably be, and I would much rather have answered it alone, without masculinity-itself Ben Bellamy, mistakable as my husband and co-host, at my side.

"Mr. Kimball, nice to see you." I stepped aside to welcome him in. "Welcome to Wildwood Lodge."

Once inside, Calder Kimball took off his double-breasted wool pea-coat, revealing—yes!—a dress shirt and a cardigan sweater with the sleeves pushed up. His thick-rimmed glasses were on point from my wish, just like Mr. Deloitte's! Oh, this was a dream coming true, and I was aware of it in the very moment of its incarnation.

He might not have the fair hair and ice-blue eyes of the fair-haired Mr. Deloitte—Mr. Kimball was dark and handsome instead—but he was the hot-nerd fantasy I'd been cultivating all these years, right down to his instant focus on the bookshelf.

Instead of me.

"Wow. That is one impressive bookcase." Calder Kimball walked straight for the shelves of dusty books.

Seneca sidled up to me and in *sotto voce* said, "That's one impressive history teacher."

Yeah. Totally.

She went back in the kitchen. We followed, and Calder gravitated toward the bookshelf in the kitchen.

I swear, this whole house was filled with books!

Calder pulled a volume off the shelf and held it up to show me the title. "Seriously? I just read this one." He came and stood by me. Mm. He smelled like sawdust and Old Spice. "Nils Ogleby, the author, knows more than any other living person about Alexander the Great.

36

Did you know Alexander's father was assassinated at the wedding of Cleopatra?"

"How awful!" I recoiled.

"Love and hate sometimes go together." He frowned, like he might be carrying a love-hate burden. *A broken heart!*

"Cleopatra of Macedon," Ben muttered near me. "Not Cleopatra Euridice of Egypt."

"There are two?" I asked.

"Of course," Ben and Calder said at the same time.

Calder gave us a brief primer on the ancient conqueror. It was interesting. And his eyes lit up when he gave some gory details about a battle where Alexander sacked Thebes.

"He certainly knows more about Alexander the Great than I do." Seneca giggled. "But I'd sign up for his class."

Me, too. Sigh.

Even if he hadn't fallen at my feet to say I was the long-lost student he'd been looking for, he was still delicious, and mysterious. Medium build, dark, very handsome with a strong nose and the whole *I'm very intelligent* vibe going on. I could definitely study hard for an A in the class on Calder Kimball.

"Jayne. Jayne!" Ben touched my elbow, and I snapped back to the present. "You all right? You looked like you were having a stroke."

"I was." I studied Calder for another moment. Was this what destiny looked like? Mmm. Very nice.

"What? Now you sound like you're eating chocolate."

"That's a good idea." I turned to Ben, who'd resumed his accustomed disdainful look toward me. I was used to it now. It felt natural. "Let's set the table for dinner, with place cards. Alphabetically." Jayne, Kimball ...

Wait, that wasn't right. I wasn't thinking straight—not a surprise.

Anyway, I was looking forward to this event a lot more now that I'd met Calder Kimball, the man my teenage first-snowfall wish had bestowed on me, wrapped in sexy tweed.

Chapter 6

Ben

Before dinner, we milled around, making introductions and small talk. Soon, the six of us sat down around the large dining room table. Seneca served us her Italian dinner—pasta, marinara sauce, crusty breadsticks, a salad with the best vinaigrette I'd eaten in a long time.

Fine, I was eating my *pasta for Christmas—gasp!* words. And they were delicious.

"This is really good," Chieko said. "I'd eat pasta all day every day if I could, but I save it for Christmas. Let's take a picture. Photos or the meal didn't happen." She whipped out her phone and snapped some of everyone. My phone beeped that she'd forwarded it to me.

"I love pasta," Lester said, looking at Chieko like he was drinking her in. "The best pasta I ever ate was in Japan, believe it or not, when I was stationed there." He told about his deployment and months in Yokohama.

Everyone else chimed in something about traveling to Asia. We shared easy conversation, even though we were strangers an hour ago.

I had to hand it to Jayne. She'd assembled a group of pleasant, like-minded people—probably by accident, like most things she accomplished. But it was looking like her accidents ended up being a lot better than most people's deliberate choices.

Why was that?

"My parents and I were in Cambodia for a few months." Jayne's eyes sparkled when she told her story of a humanitarian mission to dig wells in a rural village. "When my mom met that boa constrictor, I thought she'd jump out of her skin like a reptile does."

It wasn't the funniest story, but Jayne's laugh created some sort of chain reaction at the back of my neck, all the way down my spine, and radiated out from there. She could've won a daytime Emmy for that laugh.

"That's hilarious," Calder said as he passed her the peas, and their eyes met. Jayne's went all soft and golden brown.

All the hair stuck up on the back of my neck.

Okay, I liked this group with one exception: the know-it-all history teacher.

"It reminds me of when the British were colonizing India." Dude went into a high school history lecture on the topic, and I glazed over to the point I probably looked like Grandma Bonnie's ham.

Lester and Chieko were glued to him, and Seneca, too. I did not get it.

Seneca shivered. "I don't think we should talk snakes while we're eating linguine."

Couldn't that Kimball Caldwell, Coldcut Bimbo, or whatever his name was, notice when he was talking about something no one cared about?

Fine. I was the only one who didn't care.

The problem was, Jayne's head was tilted to the side, and she was gazing at him like he'd hung the moon.

"I've never even heard about that war between a well-armed trading company and an entire subcontinent," she said when he wound down. "That's so interesting."

"My students love when I tell that bit of history." Geek loved his topic.

"I'll bet they do." Jayne looked like she loved it too—and maybe even loved the guy telling the story. Crud! They'd just met. How could she be interested that fast? They were practically strangers. He might even be a … reprobate! Had she done a background check on all these people before they arrived?

Note to self: shoot a text to my buddy Officer Fenton at the police station back in Albany and have him run this so-called history teacher's name and legal history.

"What do you think, Ben?" Beside me, Seneca offered another breadstick. "Do you find the British conquest of India fascinating?" She lowered her voice. "Because you're giving off a fairly hostile vibe. You don't have a personal stake in it, do you? No Indian ancestors who were oppressed?"

"Call me Mr. Non-Sequitur, but I just don't think President Andrew Jackson was the man of the people that everyone claims him to be." Fine, it was off-topic from what the history guru captivating Jayne's attention had said, but it got the subject to change.

"My favorite thing about Andrew Jackson is his decision to put himself on the twenty-dollar bill." Seneca took a breadstick for herself, the crumbs falling everywhere when she crunched it. She giggled again.

At the giggle, I took a second look at Seneca. Something tired lived near the corners of her eyes, but otherwise, she was nice-looking, if quite a few years my senior.

"Okay, everyone." Jayne tapped the side of her goblet with her spoon handle. "I have a quiz for you all, which I think will make this week absolutely great—for all of us."

Cutlery was set down, and everyone listened to Jayne. She stood at her place at the head of the table and smiled. Wow, that smile. Even with a hint of marinara sauce at its edge, it was a killer.

"I'm so glad to meet you all in person at last. I've been looking forward to it for weeks, and now that you're here, I hope you'll share

40

with me something personal."

My spine stiffened. "How personal?"

A few nervous chuckles skittered around the table.

"Not like *that*." Jayne laughed in her winning way. "I want to know what would constitute a *perfect Christmas* for you. Just throw out your answers as you think of them. Hit me with them. Go!"

"Easy." Lester lifted a forkful of linguine as if it was a toast. "Pasta! My family ate pasta like it was a religious ritual every Christmas. So, you already hit my number one requirement. Thank you, and my compliments to the chef."

Seneca dipped her head. "You're welcome."

If eyes could pop out of a head, mine almost did. Jayne's random guess about pasta had been a bull's-eye win? This woman had some kind of strange magic.

Others threw out their answers.

Chieko wanted us all to ice skate—no surprise there—and to have everyone sing around the piano. I hoped everyone liked to sing, and that Jayne had planned for the right ice skate sizes.

As his second-level request after pasta, Lester wished for a fresh-cut Christmas tree and to be the one to cut it down and set it up near the fire.

Seneca wanted to cook—bless her soul—for everyone, but also to take a sleigh ride over the river and through the woods. Tricky request. It might be a little tough to arrange at the last minute.

Callum Coldwell Kildare or whatever wanted to read Dickens around the fire at night. What a boring request. Did we all have to listen while he droned on in Victorian vocabulary?

"Me?" I pointed at my chest.

"You haven't mentioned anything yet." Jayne was looking at me, and everyone else was staring, too. "What is your perfect Christmas?"

Having my grandparents with me, I could have said, but it would've dampened the mood. And I wasn't about to tell my secret wish of dancing near the Christmas tree and the fire to the song "White

41

Christmas" with a beautiful woman, or of kissing her at the end of the song. "Good classic Christmas music, I guess. Andy Williams, Bing Crosby, Dean Martin. You know the drill."

What a cop-out.

"Okay!" Jayne clapped. "All of those sound great. Let's make and decorate cookies, too."

Seneca raised a finger. "I cook, but I don't bake."

A general *me neither* rumbled around the table. Jayne's shoulders fell. It'd been the one thing she'd requested, and—

Wait, wait, wait. "I've got this." I raised my palms and lowered them to calm the panic. "Let me manage the cookie baking arrangements, if that's all right." I tapped my temple. "I've got a recipe right here."

For the first time since the history teacher entered the picture, Jayne graced me personally with one of her smiles. Despite the fact my logic was *not* interested in her, that smile enveloped me like the dawn after a dark night, and my physical body reacted. "Ben, you're a lifesaver!"

My face got hot. Please say I wasn't blushing. "It's my grandma's recipe."

"Great. Let's all give each other a perfect Christmas." She smiled at everyone, and they all clapped.

Fine, I wouldn't be dictating all the *perfect* terms of Christmas, but the things everyone had requested fit closely enough to my ideals that I wouldn't veto anything. I wasn't going to stomp on someone else's dream unless it involved something truly revolting—like karaoke to "Grandma Got Run Over by a Reindeer" for hours at a time.

Everyone stood and began clearing the table, taking dishes to the kitchen.

Teamwork wasn't a bad thing, but I wanted a little time alone with Jayne, just to clarify some points. "Okay, everyone," I said. "Let's take turns on dishes. Since Seneca is cooking, the rest of us can clean up. Jayne and I will take tonight's meal." I shooed everyone else out to the living room, where Lester laid a roaring fire.

Everyone else filtered out, and Jayne ran hot water in the sink to do dishes.

As soon as no one was looking, Jayne turned to me—her face a picture of panic, almost like that Edvard Munch guy-screaming painting. "Ben! What am I going to do? There are no ice skates on the property. And where in the world am I going to get a horse-drawn sleigh at the last minute?" She grabbed me by the biceps, digging her fingers into them.

The pain lasted a full three seconds, but then she glanced at her hands and dropped them, as if realizing she'd probably left little purple bruises. Her face reddened. "Sorry."

Not a problem. She could put her hands on me anytime. "Not sure what to do about either of those complications." Or about a chainsaw for cutting down a tree—add that to the list.

With a huge, overwhelmed sigh, she put her hands in the hot soapy water and began washing plates and stacking them for me to rinse and dry. "Ben, you're right about me, you know."

"I am?" I knew I was. "How so?" I rinsed and dried and put away the first plate.

"I'm unprepared and basically an organizational disaster."

True, but how could I confirm that aloud without sounding like a total jerk? "Well, your pasta planning worked out."

She paused and looked up at me. "It did, didn't it?" She let out another long sigh, this time less overwhelmed. "You're right. It's going to be fine."

That hadn't been what I meant, but if it calmed her down …

She talked on about all the fun things everyone wanted to do, and I half-listened, half-ruminated. It was pretty amazing of her to simply blat out her worries to me, as if I were a close friend, or a sounding-board. A confidant.

I'd always been able to get people to talk sports and sports-related background stories to me, which was why I'd gone into psychology, but

43

I'd never reciprocated and told anyone *my* misgivings or doubts.

Suddenly, I wanted to tell her about Grandma and Grandpa, about Christmas with them, about why I felt so compelled to make all of the things right.

But I'd never told anyone. Not anyone.

Why did I ache to tell my heart's secret to Jayne Renwick?

Chapter 7

Jayne

"Okay," I said the next morning over breakfast. "Our first activity of the day is getting Lester his tree." Then we could fire up the hot glue guns and make some ornaments out of pine cones we collect.

"What's Christmas without a tree?" Lester stuffed his last bite of pancakes in his mouth. "We have to have a tree. I'll chop it down."

Someone was playing the piano—very well. I headed into the living room to find Chieko at the keys playing Christmas tunes. "Duet?" I asked and sat beside her. We did "Winter Wonderland" together from my duets book. It was really fun.

Lester and Seneca walked up.

"Can we sing?" Seneca asked. "I'm not very good, but I love the Christmas songs."

Who didn't? "Of course! Pick a favorite. I'm guessing Chieko can play everything."

Chieko could, and Seneca chose "Up on the Housetop," "Santa Claus is Coming to Town," and "O Little Town of Bethlehem."

Then, Lester chose some favorites, and even Calder added to the list.

"I like the historical favorites—you're probably not surprised," he said, setting the songbook in front of Chieko, open to the page with "God Rest Ye, Merry Gentlemen" and "The Holly and the Ivy."

We sang those next. Normally, I thought of singing carols around a piano as a nighttime activity, but morning worked just as well. In fact, it made for a great start to the day.

"I love singing the old carols," Seneca sighed. "It makes Christmas feel real to me. Like when I was a child. My mother had the nicest voice. My ex did, too." A wistful sigh followed, but she bucked up and sang again.

By then, everyone had gathered and was singing—everyone but Ben. A little thread spooled out from my chest and went looking for him. Weird, since Calder was already in the room and had joined ten songs ago.

Voices grew tired, and Lester returned to his favorite topic. "Who's ready to go choose a tree? We've got the woods nearby."

"Great idea. Real trees. More authentic." Calder looked up from the history book he'd just picked up. "Jayne wants everything perfect. Let's make that happen."

Aw, my little heart!

My gaze darted around for … never mind. I wasn't looking for Ben Bellamy.

"Authenticity is great," Calder said, "but let's also be realistic. We shouldn't use real candles like they did to light the original *tannenbaum* trees in Germany."

"Fire hazard," Seneca agreed.

This was fun. I loved watching everyone interact.

Frankly, Calder was beautiful as he led the discussion—and mentioned my needs. *He cares about what I want!* How amazing was that?

Calder was who I'd always wanted, and he was right here.

Sure, he seemed a little better suited in interests to my best friend

Mallory, who couldn't ever get enough of history conversations, but she'd wished for a prince, and I'd been the one dreaming of Mr. Deloitte.

"What we need," Lester said, craning his neck back to assess the height of the lodge's ceiling in the main living area, "is a fifteen-foot tree. Or more. Minimum fifteen feet."

"That's too high to decorate!" Seneca, so practical, bumped him aside and stood on the raised hearth. "We'll fall to our death if we try to scale the walls and put on the angel."

"Angel? Don't you mean star?" Chieko said.

Uh-oh. We might get into one of those *star-versus-angel* tree-topper arguments.

"No, we won't." Calder looked up from the book he held open. "There's a ladder. I saw it in the shed out back, looking to see whether they had any more boxes of books stored away." The guy smiled.

Thanks, Calder. Good save.

"Then it's settled." Lester pushed a sofa aside, and made a space for a tree. "We'll put it right here. Jayne, my friend, where's your chainsaw?"

"Chainsaw? I—I'm not sure." Instinct told me to smack myself in the forehead. Like I'd told Ben last night doing dishes, I was a walking disaster. I'd planned for crocheted toilet-seat covers, but not a way to cut down a fresh tree. "Did you see one in the shed, Calder?"

Please, Calder—save me!

At that moment, Ben walked in. "Did someone say chainsaw?"

"I doubt we need one." Calder shut his book and stepped closer to me, squaring his shoulders protectively between me and Ben. "There's a logger's saw, the two-man kind, out in the tool shed. Lester and I can use it in tandem. And I saw a hatchet as well."

"That's fine." Ben raised and dropped a shoulder. A nice, sizeable shoulder. I darted a glance at it, and then at the biceps I'd clung to out of desperation last night. Rock solid. "If you change your mind, let me know."

47

"Change our minds about what?" Chieko's hands came off the piano keys. "Do you have a chainsaw?"

"Out in my truck's cab. But if you'd rather use the manual saw just to get back to your pioneer pilgrim whatever roots, that's fine. I get it. Whatever constitutes a perfect Christmas for people, I'm supporting it." He darted me a look. The blue of his eyes was intense, penetrating, *hot video*.

"A power tool would be fantastic." Lester hustled out to Ben's truck with him, traipsed back through the living room with the bright orange saw, and gave a wide *come along* wave. "Let's go choose our perfect tree."

Everyone put on coats and boots, and we followed him into the woods. Lester's perfect Christmas requirement was on its way.

I trailed at the back of the company. "Where did the chainsaw come from?" I asked Ben, who'd fallen back and matched my pace. "Did you really bring one from home?"

"So you didn't notice that I missed breakfast?"

"I thought you were taking your sole opportunity in life to sleep in." At our news studio, no one slept in. Even the nightly news anchors often started their days at three a.m. or earlier for promo spots to be filmed. "Where were you instead?"

"Tool rental business in the next town."

What? But the next town was a forty-minute drive. "You went all the way over there?"

"And in case it occurs to you to panic about this, I also grabbed us a cutting permit for the tree."

Permit. Ugh. Another detail I'd overlooked. "Thanks, Ben." I glanced up at him, and he shot me a sidelong smile.

Oh, his smile was deadly. My knee buckled on the next step. If I hadn't been all about Calder Kimball today, I would have taken that smile as a genuine bit of flirtation from none other than Ben Bellamy.

Good night, nurse! He was ice and fire in my veins.

I'd better mind my galloping hormones. They were getting ahead of themselves when it came to Ben Bellamy.

***

The six of us hiked out into the forest near Wildwood Lodge.

"All this snow is really something." Seneca, whose legs were shorter even than Chieko's, had a hard time keeping up. "We never get this much snow in the city."

The elevation might bring the deeper snowfall.

"If it would help, Seneca, you can walk in my steps." Calder positioned himself in front of her. "I'll take smaller strides."

Oh, he was a gem. Truly. One chamber of my heart kind of exploded as Calder walked in such a way that Seneca's struggle lessened.

"There's enough snow," Lester said, "we could build an igloo. Or a snow cave. We did that at a winter survival camp I was in for the military one year. Out in the state of Washington." He told about that a bit as we trekked.

"We did that same activity at a skating retreat in Montreal once." Chieko was walking beside Lester. "This is the perfect snow for igloo-building. It's heavy but still packable."

We entered the forested area, not too far from the cabin.

"I love that tree." Chieko stopped, pointing at a beautiful fir tree. "Do you all love it, too?"

Lester walked all the way around it. "It's great. Full all the way around."

"And a good height, too," I said.

"It will balance the room," Calder said.

"Just one problem." Ben aimed the tip of the chainsaw at a spot halfway up. "See that?"

Two little heads poked out of a nest.

"Pigeons? In the forest? I thought they exclusively were city-dwellers." Seneca waved to them. "They're so cute. And listen, they're cooing."

"Mourning doves," Ben said. "My grandma loved them. She

recorded their songs in the mornings sometimes." He turned to me. "She would have loved this moment."

We paused, listening, as the birds' sad cooing continued.

"Well, we will have to choose another tree," I declared. We couldn't have Ben's grandma's favorite birds disturbed.

And how sweet that he knew her favorite bird.

"This one is almost as perfect," Lester declared, finding a spruce with full branches—and no nests. "Do you like it?" he asked Chieko.

"It looks great. Just like from a photograph. In fact, I'll take a photo, it's that good." She did. "And it's almost being crowded out by these other trees." Since she approved, Lester gave the thumbs up.

Calder took the hatchet and cleared away some of the lower branches for access. Then, Lester and Ben took turns with the chainsaw. Wow, the lumberjack look really suited Ben. Plaid flannel with a down vest was the new three-piece suit. Mmm.

Seneca, Chieko, and I unfolded the tarp we'd brought from the shed and spread it out.

"Timber!" Lester cut the engine on the saw and gave the trunk a final shove with his foot.

The tree fell with a bounce and a few sprinkles of needles and tufts of snow. The air was suddenly scented with balsam of the pungent sap, and I almost felt a little sad to see it felled.

But Chieko was right—it'd been crowded out, and another spruce like it had some dying sections from lack of sunlight. This way it could bring Christmas joy.

"I'm so in love with this tree," Chieko said as we dragged it over the snow on the tarp. "It's perfect, like when I was a kid."

"Me, too." Lester smiled at her. Something supernatural was happening between the two of them.

"What about you, Jayne?" Calder asked. "Is this like trees you had as a kid?"

Ben grumped a few feet away. He obviously thought very little of my childhood Christmas traditions. Truthfully, so did I.

50

"My parents didn't go in much for the trappings of the holidays."

"Nothing to make the season bright?" Seneca asked.

I shrugged, trying to seem nonchalant. But they'd all see right through me. "I guess because I was the caboose kid, they were kind of worn out on big holiday celebrations. I'm fifteen years younger than my next older sister. The four of them were born in a herd, and then I was this afterthought. About the time they all moved out, Mom and Dad decided Christmas was for service to others."

"It is," said Chieko. "They're not wrong."

"Oh, for sure," I agreed. "But their idea of service was performing humanitarian aid in countries like Mali, Bangladesh, and Nicaragua. I went with them every year, and we dug wells or built schools. It was a great way to live."

Ben, who was now beside me, cleared his throat. "Either that explains something, or else it's a dichotomy."

For sure, he'd think that. Like my family, Ben considered my obsession with all the Christmas trappings frivolous. "I like fancy stuff. You're right. I'm probably trying to compensate." Okay, I was totally trying to compensate.

"Well"—Chieko gave me a side-hug—"we'll do our best to make up for it this year. You'll get your perfect Christmas, Jayne."

"Yeah," a few voices chimed.

My throat tightened, and my chin trembled. "Thanks," I managed, my voice small. "That means a lot to me." It meant everything, actually.

Once inside the toasty lodge, and after we'd had a cup of cocoa, we set up the tree.

Then, it was time to decorate.

"We'll need the ladder to add lights and ornaments to the higher-up areas." The tree was a lot taller inside the lodge. "I can go out and get it." I headed for the back door, grabbing my parka.

"Let me go with you." Ben was at my side in a minute.

"No, I can go." Calder slipped his feet into his boots. "I'm the one who's most familiar with the shed. Let me do it. You probably need to get the chainsaw returned to the rental shop before dark."

Ben glanced at the cuckoo clock over the mantel. He frowned and conceded he should go. "Don't put too many lights on without me." He left.

I followed Calder outside for supplies.

In the shed, I held the flashlight, while Calder chose among the three ladders leaning against the wall.

"You seem pretty familiar with tool sheds."

"Yep. It's been my whole life until a couple of years ago. My parents are ... builders." He shot me a wary look, as if I might violate him by trying to dig out some terrible secret.

I didn't need to ferret out any terrible secrets. "That's great. Builders. Better than being tear-er downers." Were those actual words? I sounded like a loon.

"They do some of that, too. Demolition is part of the territory."

"You don't want to spend Christmas with them?" There. I'd gone right for the ferreting. Cringe!

"Don't get me wrong. They're the best people on earth. I just needed ... some space."

Okay. I guess I could understand that. It seemed my family needed some space from me, too. My stomach hurt. "I'd better go inside and check on things"—before I told Calder what a loser my family thought I was.

Chapter 8

Ben

I returned the chainsaw to the shop, and then I sped back to Wildwood Lodge. If the group didn't wait for me to help decorate the tree, I'd be hard-pressed not to get up in the night and fix things.

Because they'd need to be fixed, if Jayne's decorating taste made its way onto the branches and boughs. Good grief. Did everything she brought need to be branded merchandise from a movie or a TV show? There was nothing about a red robot action figure that held reference to a holy night in Bethlehem.

The return to the lodge caught me again with the magnificence of the view. Now that the place was inhabited, and with smoke piping out the chimney, it was even more appealing. My foot relaxed on the gas, and I tooled down the drive instead of speeding, just taking in the idyllic scene of the logs and the windows and the warmth among the cold of the mountain setting.

"Hey, I'm back." I kicked the snow off my boots and went inside, breath held, and hoping that no one had ruined our perfect tree with purple plastic cat ornaments or …

"I hope it's okay, but we went ahead and strung all the lights."
Seneca came up beside me. Music played—and not annoying pop
songs, even. Bless these people. "Jayne said you brought all those
strands. It turned out to be just enough."

No patch or branch lacked a glinting twinkle. "You covered it," I
said, walking closer. It'd been partially decorated, and it looked
amazing.

Jayne stood halfway up the ladder, looking pretty in the glow of
the lights.

"I'm kind of an expert," Seneca went on. "I'm a nurse. I think of
unlit branches like a wound, and of the twinkle-light strands as
bandages." The cooking fanatic laughed. "Don't say it's overkill. I
won't hear of it."

Not overkill for my taste. "It looks like you found the rest of my
boxes."

"You're *Grandma?*" Lester brought a mostly empty tote of the
ornaments I'd brought—labeled with the word *Grandma* on the side.
"Should I be surprised?" He let out a *haw-haw* that shook the rafters.
"Great codename if you ever want to be a spy."

Jayne climbed the ladder. "Can you hand me a few glass
ornaments?"

Um, no? "You're not asking for the *Revengers* set that you
brought, I hope." I picked up a box of Grandma's prettiest antique gold
and white glass balls, adding a hook to the ornament that was missing
one.

"I just want to do what the group likes." She shrugged, placing a
decoration in a bare spot. "It's part of my everyday job description to
know my audience. Yours too."

True. "Then, as your audience, I vote no *Revengers.*"

"The audience is always right." She placed one of Grandma
Bonnie's Victorian baubles on a branch.

Speaking of audiences, just then I was totally Jayne Renwick's as
she perched like some kind of beautiful bird on the ladder, her arms

stretching out and placing the delicate glass orbs on branch after branch. Like a dancer, her movements were fluid, mesmerizing.

I handed her a few more pieces, and then I placed my own first piece. The music changed to a Bing Crosby song—not "White Christmas," but "Happy Holiday," which was almost as good. The moment sprinkled over me like snow crystals.

This was a good Christmas.

Perfect?

I couldn't say quite yet, but the tree's evergreen scent and the good music and the warm fire approximated perfection anyway.

Seneca snapped some photos of all of us near the tree.

Seriously, it was the most unlikely thing I could have imagined— that Product Placement Jayne was creating a picturesque holiday *for me.*

Chapter 9

Jayne

"The lighting turned out gorgeous on the tree." Seneca settled heavily into the leather lounge chair beside the Christmas tree. "That, plus the fire, gives this room the perfect ambience. It's almost romantic." She shot a loving glance at Ben.

Uh-oh. It seemed like Seneca was trying for a little romance herself. I mean, Lester and Chieko had paired off. They were sharing the loveseat, and a person would have been hard-pressed to wedge a thin dime between them.

I'd sat dangerously close to Calder when I plopped down, and he'd been forced to lift an arm across the back of the sofa—around me.

I wasn't born yesterday. I knew a few tricks.

Calder had buried his nose in Dickens, the first fiction I'd seen him crack open. "This is a good part." He cleared his throat, quoting from the page he was open to. "No space of regret can make amends for one life's opportunity misused."

"Very deep." Ben sat down on the other side of me, hogging almost half the couch with his shoulders. A wave of his cologne wafted over me, fresh and clean. I had to turn my head toward Calder to keep from getting locked into it and trailing after him like one of those floating-helplessly cartoon creatures drawn by the steam of a roast turkey dinner.

"Have you missed opportunities?" Seneca asked. "I have."

Everyone nodded, kind of wincing.

"No one gets out of this life without at least a few regrets." Calder thumbed the pages of his book.

This was not the discussion I wanted to have in front of a cozy fire. No regrets, just joyous moments. "Who'd like some hot cocoa tonight? I have candy canes we can use to stir them and make mint cocoa."

"I love mint cocoa." Chieko stood up. "I'll go make some for everyone."

Calder read on, not really paying attention to me, or to the fact his arm was around me. When it was time to turn the page, he did it with one hand.

That was a good sign, right?

I could engage him on the topic of Dickens. I liked Dickens. I'd seen a lot of film adaptations on BBC with Mallory. Unlike Calder's history lesson last night at dinner that might as well have happened on an alien planet, for all I knew about the British East India Company.

But if I were with him, my life would be full of delightful details about the past, making connections, feeling smarter about the world.

If snowfall wishes were to be trusted, this was meant to be.

And yet, Ben's aftershave ...

"Let's watch a movie." Ben extracted himself from the far end of the sofa and found my stack of movies on the mantel, where I'd left them. Everyone's favorites. "Where should we start? *A Christmas Carol?* That's your favorite, right?" He shot a poisoned arrow of a look at Calder. Why all the hostility? Calder had found the ladder, he'd helped Seneca walk in snow. He was a great guy.

Is Ben ... jealous?

Not possible. He was Ben Bellamy. He was basically a TV station divinity. He wasn't interested in me. He thought I had bad taste.

My gut said otherwise.

"That'd be great." Calder leaned forward, taking his arm from around me. "If I were at home with my parents, we'd never slow down to watch a movie. Wait. Which version is it? George C. Scott?"

"Of course George C. Scott," I said. Calder had been specific in his questionnaire. My personal favorite was the Muppets version.

Chieko brought us each a cup of cocoa, complete with a peppermint stick. Mmm. Delicious. That, plus the roaring fire that Lester had built—wow. This moment was one to soak into, just like I'd seen on TV and in movies, where everything was the picture of enjoyment.

Calder sipped from his mug. "The one with George C. Scott is the only true version. Pop it in, would you, Ben? The costuming and sets are brilliant with the whole feel of the Victorian Era."

"My high school friend Mallory did her master's thesis on architecture of the Victorian and Edwardian eras." There! I'd added something non-ignorant to the history-related conversations. Score!

"Is that right?" For the first time, Calder looked vitally interested in something I'd said. His eyes sparkled in the lights from the tree. "How fascinating. Where does she live? I'd love to have her come give my classes a bonus lecture when we cover nineteenth-century England."

"Boston," I said, though it wasn't fully correct, since Mallory moved around a lot, and I didn't know where she was for her work as a historical architecture consultant these days. *I wonder if she'll ever get her first-snowfall wish for a prince, or if Emily will get a proposal from a valiant hero on a bridge.*

The movie started, and Lester hushed everyone. "No commentary in movies. It's a military rule."

Dang. Just when I was connecting with Calder. I missed having his arm around me. If I scooted a little he might just—

Ben returned to the sofa with a heavy plunk—a lot closer to me than he had sat earlier. In fact, his weight pulled the cushion downward at the point where I was sitting. Gravity tilted me toward him. He really was a muscular, solid guy. My own gravity seemed to be pulling my body in his direction, too. *But, Calder is right here!*

Calder stirred his cocoa with the candy cane as the credits rolled and the action began. "The carolers are singing an authentic English tune from pre-Victorian days, and they get the harmonies just right. That's one of the reasons I love this film."

"Shush," Lester warned.

Nerd obsession or none, Calder was really cute. I could imagine Mallory and Calder going on for hours on these topics, which would make friend get-togethers after Calder and I were married great. He got into the movie.

I couldn't. The fire crackled. I kept staring at it instead of the movie. My senses were all high-jacked by something—someone—else. Even over the heavenly scent of the burning pine logs, all I could smell was Ben. All I could feel was his nearness. The fire mesmerized me, telling me I was alone here with Ben Bellamy. Everyone else had faded.

Ben coughed, and I snapped to life again. However, then he angled toward me, placing his feet on the coffee table. Then, he yawned, extending his arms and laying one on the sofa behind me, right where Calder's had been a few minutes ago.

"You don't mind, do you?" Irish Spring mingled with his cologne and some other manly scent. It swirled in the air around me. "Gotta stretch out for this movie."

"It's all right." The weight of his arm kidnapped my brainpower. "I don't mind." I relaxed against the back of the couch, and Ben's pheromones enveloped me.

Across in the recliner, Seneca was looking at her phone. She looked distressed—but not about any of us. Her thoughts appeared to be far away from Wildwood Lodge.

The first ghost visited Ebenezer Scrooge, and beside me, on my right, Calder mouthed the dialogue between young Ebenezer and his boss, Fezziwig. It was endearing. The history-loving hottie really did love this historical holiday movie—and I'd given him the chance to watch it and, in a small way, to have a more-perfect Christmas.

I glanced at Ben, and he was looking at me, not at the movie. His upper lip had this perfect cupid's bow to it, complementing the square line of his jaw. A light scruff of blond beard covered his chin—something that never happened while he was at the station. WGWG required clean shaves.

As if controlled by something besides my good sense, my hand rose. My knuckles grazed his beard's stubble. Ben's eyes drifted shut at my touch. He licked his lips.

I dropped my hand. "Sorry."

Ben reached for my hand and placed my palm flat against his chin. "Vacation. I forgot my razor."

He should forget it more often. Under his strong arm's power, my palm roughed back and forth along that scruff, and then he laid my hand back in my lap—where it pulsated.

I made a fist. The aftereffects didn't wane.

Beside me, Calder laughed at the movie's script, the part about the game of analogies. It should have awakened me to the fact I was flirting with the wrong man, but I couldn't take my eyes off Ben, who now riveted his gaze on the movie—but with a faint, triumphant smile toying with the side of his oh-so-kissable mouth.

Chapter 10

Jayne

Skating day! I bolted upright in bed after a not-so-wholesome dream of skating with Ben Bellamy. The thing that had my heart pounding should have been the illicit dream-embrace, but no.

Instead, it was my complete lack of skates for my guests.

How could I have done this to myself?

"What am I going to do?" I moaned aloud and curled tighter in a ball under my Rainbow Brite's Merry Christmas bedspread. I'd themed each room. Ben had taken the sock-monkey- Santa room next door to my 1980s cartoon room. "Think, Jayne, think."

But thinking wouldn't solve the fact that ice skating was on the slate today and we had zero ice skates.

Where was I going to find six pairs of skates? None were in the shed or the house or anywhere. I'd scoured the property.

"Your failure to plan is a perennial problem," I said to myself as I headed to the hallway shower with my towel in hand. "It's affecting others now. It's ruining the perfect Christmas."

All the rooms besides mine had bathrooms attached, but I had taken the Rainbow Brite room so the other guests could have private baths.

I tuned on the water as hot as it would go. Steam billowed. I stood under the shower until my skin practically wrinkled, but no solution appeared. When I finally toweled off and reached for my underthings, sweater, and jeans—

Great.

And, of course, I'd left everything I needed to wear back in my room.

Brilliant.

And the clothes I'd removed had strayed too close to the shower. They were sopping wet. I wrung them out in the sink, but no way could I put manage getting them back over my body.

And there was only the small towel I'd grabbed instead of a bath sheet. Even better. This day just got better and better.

Willing the towel to stretch, I wrapped up as tightly as possible to cover myself and dripped out into the hall.

"Oof!" *Naturally*, I ran straight into Ben Bellamy. "Oh, my gosh." I nearly dropped the towel.

Ben's gaze crawled over me from wet-mop of hair to gold-painted toenails and back to my eyes.

"Good morning." He didn't suppress a wolfish chuckle. "Are we spending time in the Jacuzzi today? You're just giving us a preview of how wrinkled we'll look on exit?"

"It was a lengthy shower, I know."

"You missed breakfast."

"I did?" Wow, I hadn't thought I'd been in there that long. "Some hostess. First the ice-skates debacle, and now ignoring everyone for the daily mealtime and activity plan announcement." My head fell backward, and my long hair dripped onto the backs of my ankles. "I should go get dressed."

"What ice-skates debacle?" Ben asked, stepping alongside me in the hallway. It was not a two-people-across hallway. His bicep bumped against my bare shoulder. Did he not know how uncomfortable I was, wearing only a towel, and no makeup, and with soaked-frog hair?

Frogs don't have hair. That's how uncomfortable I was—to come up with that analogy.

Then his question hit me. I paused at my bedroom door, not going in yet. "Excuse me? What did you just ask?"

"Ice-skates debacle. Explain?"

"Can I get dressed first, before we discuss?"

"Wouldn't you rather clear it up, and not wait? You seemed distressed a minute ago, and I don't like to prolong your agony." His eyes did one of those vertical scans of me again.

"But you do love to prolong my agony, Ben."

"In this moment, your agony is my ecstasy, I'll have to admit."

A host of neurons chose this moment to fire at will inside me. "Ben!"

He chuckled. "Sorry. You set up the punch line. I couldn't leave it unused. That'd be inconsiderate."

I went into my bedroom and shut the door. I heard a *thunk* against it from the other side.

"While you're dropping that towel, I'll just talk to you through the door. We can operate that way. You're dropping it, right? I mean, you'll get dressed quickly, right?"

Ugh. If we'd been at work, he would've gotten slapped with harassment charges. But as it was, I probably deserved it, too—considering I'd touched his face and ogled his upper lip at length. Plus, I dreamed about some other things last night that I was too much of a lady to discuss.

"Ben. Just say what you want to say." I did drop the towel and skittered into my clothes.

"But are you putting on your clothes now?"

"Ben." Dressed at last, I swung the door open. Then, I straightened my sweater, which had not quite made it down over my ... everything. "Excuse me. Just say what you're saying about the skates."

63

The laughter in his blue eyes had turned them more the color of the sea off the Amalfi Coast than a Swiss glacier. "You missed him, but while you were showering"—he cleared his throat—"my buddy Marcellus stopped by."

Marcellus? There was probably only one Marcellus in upstate New York. "Marcellus Dewing? The hockey coach?"

"You watch my show." Ben turned his chin like he'd just discovered a deeply held secret. "I'm guessing you saw my interview with Marcellus last week, so you recognize the name."

"Maybe." Totally. And I'd rewound it three times and paused on Ben's smile. I'd set as my phone wallpaper for a day the moment when Ben had laughed showing all his teeth. "I mean, we're sort of expected to support each other's shows as employees at WGWG, right?" No one at the station had made such a request. "Why would Marcellus Dewing come to Wildwood Lodge?"

We descended the open-railing stairway into the living area, where everyone was gathered around the coffee table in the living area—trying on shoes.

Wait! Not just any shoes. Shoes with ice skating blades on the bottom.

"Ben!" I whirled on him. "What in the world?"

"The guy owed me a favor." Ben shrugged. "He's in tight with all the skate dealers."

"Big time," Lester hollered. As I came closer, Lester went on. "Appearing on Ben's 'Beyond the Bench' show resuscitated Dewing's career. Everyone knows that."

I turned to Ben, the question in my eyes, *explain?*

"I gave an in-depth analysis of his coaching decisions, based on a psychological study of his players' history, his own coaching history, and the personality of the team's owner."

"I did see that. You said he'd made the choices in the most logical order, and then you predicted that they'd lead to a chain reaction of improved morale in the team, and a winning streak for at least the next three games."

Lester stood up on his skates, blades pressing into the hardwood floors. Yikes. "Yep, and when that happened, Marcellus didn't lose his job." He sat down and untied the laces. "Ben saved the guy's career—which had been on the chopping block. Psychology for the win."

Wow, the guy really had owed Ben a favor. "And he brought skates?" The favor Ben called in was ... *for me.*

"I got sizes for everyone's feet last night after dinner."

"I didn't hear that conversation."

"I looked at their shoes. Marcellus rounded up hockey and figure skates for everyone, their choice."

Not just one but two pairs for each person!

Ben Bellamy, my hero—again? The chainsaw, the movie last night, and now the skates arranged by calling in a favor. I shook my head slowly. "I keep saying the same two words to you, it seems."

"I don't get tired of hearing them."

I went ahead and said them. "Thanks, Ben."

"You're welcome."

"I was wondering how we were going to clear it," Chieko said. "I had my snow-shovel at the ready. Now I don't have to flex nearly as many muscles. Thanks, Ben."

I looked at him for an explanation.

He gave a small shrug. "Marcellus also arranged to scrape the snow off the pond and brought a Zamboni to smooth it. It's all ready for us."

"No way!" I threw my arms around him and said them right in his ear. "Thanks, Ben." I whispered them again. "Thanks, Ben."

Then, I suddenly got inexplicably hot. Maybe we were standing too close to the fire. I sprang away from Ben, whose face was in a filtered haze, and also looked a little goofy.

"Irrational exuberance." I straightened my sweater and went to choose my skates. "Who's ready for the ice?"

Calder descended the stairs with a pair of skates with laces tied hanging over his shoulder. "I am!"

***

"Beautiful," Seneca breathed.

"Absolutely," I breathed back.

Totally gorgeous. Our fresh tracks marred the snow banks around the pond, but it was still as picturesque as anyone could dream. Stark-branched trees rimmed the far side. Pure white surrounded the dark ice, with plenty of room to loop the edges or make figure-eights in the center.

I brushed snow off a fallen log and sat down to lace up my figure skates.

"The ice looks solid, but you can never tell by simple looks." The last thing I needed was to lose someone into bone-freezing water through a crack in the ice.

"The past forty-five days"—Calder said, staring at his phone in analysis mode, and looking extra cute as he nerded out—"temperatures have been below fifteen degrees at night, and no daytime temperatures have climbed past twenty-eight. This pond should be rock solid." He looked at me for approval, and then he stepped out onto it. Not a squeak of insolvency. "Besides, there's the obvious: it held a Zamboni."

True! How could I forget?

"Let's skate." I slipped out onto the ice, spinning once and pausing for Calder to join me, since everyone else was still lacing up. "Do you know how?"

Calder ventured out with some level of competence, but he didn't catch my offered hand. He headed for the center of the pond.

I followed, but I glanced back.

Ben paused at the side, fiddling with a speaker, which must be Blue-toothed to his phone.

I met Calder in the middle. "Are you enjoying Wildwood Lodge?"

"Can I let you in on a secret? Don't hate me for this, but I generally don't like Christmastime."

"But this year?"

66

"Is so much better than last year."

I'd take that. No effusions of a *perfect Christmas,* but I'd take a verdict of improvement.

"Care to talk about your dislike of the season?" I didn't want to pry, but … I wanted to pry. I was a reporter, after all. Sort of.

"Everything you've prepared here, Jayne, has taken my mind off the past perfectly."

Ka-ching! The hoped-for *perfect.* "Yeah? What have you liked?"

"The movie last night was classic, and the library in the lodge! It's a history teacher's version of heaven."

I'd be in my version of heaven if he'd just tell me a little more about what had hurt him in the past to make him resist the most wonderful time of the year.

"I'll be honest, Calder. I haven't read as many of those books as I should have."

"That's okay." For a minute he tilted his head to the side, back in analysis mode. It reminded me of the time I told Mallory the only history book I'd ever read was *Gone with the Wind.* And that maybe I'd only watched the movie. She had not been impressed. Again, I had to push away the thought that Calder would really like Mallory.

Finally, he smiled at me again. "I never expect anyone to have read all the books I've read. I'm kind of obsessed." His dark eyes had a fire in them. "Again, I have to thank you. For everything."

Chieko swooped around us in circles, lapping us all. Seneca wasn't bad, and Lester had some pretty good moves. He could skate fast—and he could flip around and keep his momentum while skating backward. Soon, he and Chieko were pair-skating. I mean, she was by far his superior, but he wasn't tripping her or anything.

"Come on, Ben." Seneca put on some speed. "You're missing out."

"Just setting up some music for us." Soon, classic Christmas songs came over the speaker—the kind Ben had described as his favorites—from a bygone era. I'd heard them here and there on the radio and in stores while shopping, but none held real nostalgia for me, other than

"Rudolph," which I'd sung in grade school as the starring role with the red nose.

"Ben, hustle. I'm leaving you in the dust—or frost." Seneca lapped him—she skated around the pond's edge twice before Ben had made it once. "I thought you were a sports guy. You look surprisingly wobbly."

"I'm not wobbling. I'm getting my sea legs."

"This sea is solid, dude."

My attention on Calder's mysterious dislike of last Christmas slipped as I sneaked glances at Ben, who clung to the rink's edge. Hadn't he ever skated? He seemed so much like the guy who'd done every sport. In upstate New York, the definition of *every sport* would obviously include high school hockey teams or at least community clubs. How had he escaped learning to skate?

"We should skate," Calder said. He held out a hand.

I looked at Calder, and then at Ben in total klutz-mode, then back at Calder.

Seneca skated up, a breeze in her super-curly hair. "Race you, teacher-man." She crouched, and he took the bait.

"Sure, nurse-woman. First to the far side doesn't have to do dishes tonight."

They were off!

I turned back to Ben, who'd finally made it away from the side. "Whoa." His arms rowed backward. "I'm here. I've got it."

"Take my hands," I said, and he accepted both of them.

His spine straightened, and his shoulders relaxed. "Thanks."

"Good music choices." I pulled him along. He wobbled some, but he made progress at last. "You really like the oldies."

"You mean the goodies."

"Okay." I folded my fingertips around his. "Are there baddies?"

"Too many to count." He named a few. "But the worst one is the reindeer that killed the grandma."

"Is that anyone's favorite?"

"I don't know, but maybe I don't have much of a sense of humor about it. I think it should be banned in every country by order of law."

"Strong opinion," I said. "Other than the existence of that song, how's your Christmas going?" Because he'd been so determined that I'd fail to provide his *perfect Christmas* standard, his assessment of the events so far mattered to me more than anyone else's. "Is it as bad as you expected?"

"You make it sound like I'm this harsh critic." He met my eyes. "Okay, so maybe I started out that way."

"And?"

"And … let's say you know your audience a little better than I expected."

If he meant himself, then I'd take the compliment. A small compliment from Ben meant more than a thousand gushes from any of the others.

"Best day ever." Chieko sailed around him, adding a pirouette. "Sunshine, beautiful ice, mountain scenery, excellent company. This is amazing."

Lester floated past, skating like he'd done it all his life. "Agreed." He paused and snapped a photo of all of us then took a panoramic shot of the whole scene. "I'll text it to you, Jayne. Great call, getting the Zamboni."

I had Ben to thank for that—for this whole day, really.

"Why are you such a great skater, Lester?" I couldn't help asking—at risk of making Ben feel bad. *That guy could not skate.*

"Hockey team," Lester said. "All through high school."

"For real?" Chieko asked, slicing up toward him again, ice shaving into a little pile at the base of her blades when she stopped. "Let's see your speed, hockey guy."

Lester folded his arms over his chest. "I don't think so." Then, he crouched and took off like a shot.

They moved like lightning compared to the previous race between Calder and Seneca.

"Don't you dare challenge me to a race." Ben reached forward and took my elbows, and I grabbed his. "And don't tell a soul."

"Don't worry." I skated backward, and he skated forward. We completed our first lap. "Wait a minute, don't tell a soul what?"

Calder roared up beside us—careening. He lunged forward in a skating motion, but his skate slid too far, and he ended up on the ice in a twisted mass.

"Calder!" I skated to where he'd slid, reached for him, but I fell smack-dab on top of him. Ben fell on my back. We were a dog-pile of humanity.

"Oof! Jayne!" Calder scooted, but we were practically crushing him. "Are you okay?"

"Me? Yeah, what about you? I'm so sorry, Calder." I tried to pull myself off him for a moment, until a strong arm lifted me aloft. "Ups-a-daisy," I said.

I spun around and into Ben's arms, who'd already righted himself.

"Are you all right?" asked Ben.

"Calder's the one who's hurt."

"I've got this." Seneca skated up like a pro. "Nurse here. Come on, Kimball. Let's check out that wound."

"I'm not wounded. This blood's nothing. I once got in a fight with a band-saw." He lifted the back of his hand. Whoa, nasty scar.

"Oh, but you are," Seneca said.

Sure enough, the blood was blossoming at the right knee of his jeans, turning the fabric a dark burgundy.

"There's a first aid kit inside. I made sure of its location during check-in." Seneca escorted him to the far side of the pond, where she removed his skates, put on his boots, and then helped him balance. "I'll bandage you, and we'll talk again about your family."

They hobbled around the pond toward the lodge.

"Should we end the skating?" Lester hollered to them as they shrank in the distance. "It's not polite to leave a soldier behind and keep having a good time while one of us can't."

"Merely a flesh wound," Calder called.

"He'll be fine," Seneca said, "and we'll come skate again. Just keep up the fun. We'll be back."

Mortifying. Completely mortifying. I'd not only disappointed Calder with my poor reading prowess, I'd wounded him—literally—by planning the skating activity. "Sorry, Calder," I called, but they were too far across the frosted meadow now to hear.

Lester and Chieko shot around and around the pond. Meanwhile, Ben and I more or less shuffled across the ice, bumping into each other often enough that we just began to hold hands. It was organic, I swear.

And Calder wasn't here to see and get the wrong idea.

I might be getting the wrong idea. In the light filtering through the clouds today, Ben Bellamy looked like Mr. Deloitte more than ever. The blue of his eyes softened.

"To parrot your question to Lester, why are you so good at skating?" Ben asked.

"Me? In case you haven't noticed, I'm no Chieko Parsons." The very comparison! "I've only had two lessons, with exactly two takeaways: use the toe-picks on the front of one skate to propel your other foot forward in a glide."

"And the other?"

"I guess there was only one tip."

"Like this?" He attempted to follow my tip, with actually good results. "I get it. Look at that." He looked up at me, his grin in the exact broad teeth-reveal as I'd saved on my phone. "Why do you look so astounded? Because I could improve so much with one lesson?"

It was a good thing he'd chosen figure skates instead of hockey skates. Hockey skates had no toe pick.

"Because you asked for advice—and then applied it." Men, in my experience—certainly not in my athlete-dating experience with Peter, José, and the like—didn't ask for advice. "I didn't expect that."

"You're not what I expected either." Honey dripped from his words. I could almost taste their sweetness, as the phrase hovered near his lips. I stared flagrantly. Was his mouth sweet, too? Would it taste

71

like this morning's waffle syrup? Or like the sweet mint of toothpaste? Or like …

Leaning toward him slightly, I caught a bit of peppermint and vanilla, and—

"You're listing to the right. Are you okay? You look like you're having a stroke again."

"I am." The way my heart pounded, there was definitely some kind of cardiac event happening inside me. "What brand of toothpaste do you use?"

"Colgate. Are you okay, Jayne?"

I would be if I could taste the peppermint vanilla. And soon. "Uh-huh."

Geez! This guy and his pheromones! They were going to be my undoing.

Not my *undoing* undoing. Please. I was not that kind of girl. Not even for Ben Bellamy.

I skated toward the edge of the pond and knelt by the speaker. "Chieko?" I called. "Do you have a song you used as your skating routine music?" All skaters did, right? I took her answer and punched it into my phone, then unhooked Ben's phone from the speaker and plugged in my own.

The beat thumped, and I sat down hard on the fallen log, safe from Ben at this distance.

Wrong. He skated over and plonked down beside me.

"Everything all right?"

"Yep." Nope. My brain was getting caught up in the attraction-chaos-blackout. "Just needed a breather." Breathing different air from his intoxicating scent.

"Are you out of toothpaste? Do you want to borrow some? I have enough to share."

Straight off his teeth and onto my own—my little chaos-driven cells begged. "It's okay." Could he hear the pounding of my heart all the way over there, one inch from me? Our thighs touched. He was

72

sitting very close, considering we had the entirety of the pond's shore to use.

No wonder all my systems were go.

"I started to tell you something before the big ice crash."

"Yeah?" Was Ben Bellamy going to tell me something personal? My insides tingled.

Ben lowered his voice, and it was in those bass zones that only R&B singers are usually allowed to use. "Will you promise to keep what I tell you locked up tight?"

My tingles dialed up ten notches. *A secret!*

"Of course." I turned to him, and I might have moistened my lips. "Tell me," I whispered. *Tell me you want to kiss me as much as I want to kiss you.*

"I'm a total klutz."

I swallowed. The chemistry-overload in me subsided, allowing for complex thought to return. "You what?"

"Can't make a basket, can't catch a pop fly, can't kick a goal. None of it. You saw me on skates."

"Come on, really? Not one sport?"

"Table tennis."

"You mean ping-pong?" Seriously? "That's ... a fun game. That would totally make you a sports god if you lived in Asia." The Chinese and Koreans took it very seriously, from what I'd heard.

"Don't call it *fun*. It's an Olympic sport." Wry crinkles formed at the edge of his eye.

Hmm. Self-deprecating Ben was even more gorgeous. My heart lurched in my chest.

"Ben, I'm having a hard time believing you're not coordinated. You're so ... built." Uh-oh. The chemistry surged again as I let my eyes do a quick rove across his chest and shoulders. "Everything about your physique screams serious athlete."

He got that goofy grin again. "Yeah?"

"Totally." He walked like a macho guy who'd just gotten off a thousand-mile motorcycle ride. Sore and bow-legged and swaggering. Athletic.

"You think I'm built?" He flexed and then laughed, clearly unaware of the dangerous cocktail of estrogen and progesterone he was mixing in my veins by doing so. "That's one thing about me. I can build muscle quickly when I work out. And, as you know, part of the job is to look right on camera."

"You look exactly right on camera every night." Was I getting breathless again? Sheesh. I needed to drop a pile of snow down the back of my sweater to cool me off. "I mean, yeah. It shows. You take care of yourself."

"Same with you. Your hair gets an extra-nice shine under the stage lighting."

My eyes bugged out. I probably looked like a squeezed plastic fish cat toy. "You've seen me on camera?"

"I've caught your morning spot a couple of times." His tone of voice implied he'd caught it quite a few times. "Have your producers ever told you to wear light blue? It's your best color."

My. Best. Color. *Ben Bellamy thinks I have a best color.*

I tried to swallow, but all my thought processes went into spasms. I was alive with him. So into him. He was near and smelled so good, like peppermint vanilla and built-muscle-man, and—

"If it ever gets out that I'm not athletic, I'll probably lose credibility with every single viewer." He chuckled, self-deprecatingly. "So, keep my secret?"

Anything you ask, I could have breathed like a devoted puppy. "You weren't that bad."

"Please. You saw me stumbling around the ice, and after we trimmed the tree, no matter how many shots I took I could never toss the stray trimmed branches into the trash from more than a foot away."

"I honestly didn't notice that."

"You sure? I could've sworn you were onto me and my secret, so I figured I might as well come clean."

"Consider it locked down tight." Anything he'd asked me in this moment, I would've promised.

"I knew I could trust you, Jayne."

Trust me! I gulped air. "Thanks." But how had he known such a thing? "I hope I can earn that trust again and again."

"You're on your way to it. The way you're running this week. I'll admit—at first, I had some worries."

"You should have. I came into this celebrating-Christmas thing blind. You've rescued me over and over."

"I just want it to work out for everyone." He looked out across the pond at where Chieko was finishing her routine with a flourish, and Lester applauded. We applauded, too. "It's important, Christmas."

"Yeah." I was starting to see why everyone revered it so much— now that I'd actually experienced a holiday tradition or two for myself. It was nice, homey, cozy. "Can I ask you, Ben? How come you're alone on Christmas?"

"You read my application. My grandparents ... died."

"I did." But it had sounded like there was more to the story, something hanging him up beyond their deaths. I'd ask that later, but my inner bloodhound was on a different trail right now. "What I was getting at was that you're a great-looking guy. A catch. You've got women practically begging to be your girlfriend after every broadcast you upload."

"Oh. Why am I *alone* alone?" He placed his hands on his bent knees. "I did have a girlfriend. She was in television, too, so I thought we'd get each other. It should've been a good match."

My heart clunked down into my stomach. But it shouldn't have! Of *course* he'd had a girlfriend. He was Ben Bellamy, most eligible bachelor in Albany. I croaked out a question. "You broke up?"

"She did. Last year, right before Christmas."

Ouch. Triple ouch.

"I'm so sorry." *Lie.* I was over-the-moon elated about that fact. If not for it, I wouldn't have been sitting here at his side. I squelched any elation, though. "Does that memory make this holiday all the harder?"

"I don't know. I haven't really celebrated the holidays in a long time."

What? Ben Bellamy? *Mr. Christmas, and it's got to be done right?* That Ben Bellamy hadn't celebrated Christmas? "Why not?"

He closed down, pulled away, and stood up.

"Hey, it's okay." I stood up, too, but I kept a safe distance. "Things happen. Holidays turn rough things into flashing neon." The girlfriend must have really been something to turn him into this tree stump. "I get it."

Ben turned toward the pond, his demeanor a little softer—like the center parts of a tree, not like the craggy bark on the trunk. "My girlfriend was great. I just wasn't ready to commit, and she didn't get that I had some things I needed to take care of before I could get fully involved. When she pushed, I pulled away, and that was that."

Clinical. Rehearsed. "Makes perfect sense," I fibbed. "Timing is everything."

Ben looked my way again, as if seeing me for the first time. "Yeah, I think you're right."

Our gazes locked. The music muffled. All I could see or hear or feel was this moment with Ben.

A voice rose over the trees from the direction of the lodge. "Guys. Calder needs to soak his knee. Let's warm up, hit the hot tub."

Lester and Chieko didn't need to be asked twice. Their skates were off and their boots on their feet in a flash. They jogged toward the house.

Uh, my hormones and I were going to make quite the stew sharing a hot tub with Ben Bellamy and his brooding sexiness. "Is that a good idea?" I asked him.

"I'm game if you are."

Chapter 11

Ben

Whatever speed I might have lacked on the ice I made up for in my race to the hot tub. I stepped into the steaming water on the deck under the fading afternoon light like I'd been told I could have a million bucks if I arrived in under five minutes.

I'd arrived in three.

I need to be with Jayne again. Our talk near the ice had been ... well, it'd been incredible. For the first time in years—maybe ever—I'd forgotten to be Fort Knox about my feelings.

Product Placement Jayne had sold me her listening ear, and I'd exchanged it for trusting her with not just one of my secrets—but with a whole slew of them.

Who am I? What is this Wildwood Lodge air doing to me?

Something was definitely in the air here. It glittered like sun off a snow field.

"Ben? Is that you?"

Her voice—I whipped my head around so fast I could have sprained my neck.

Whoa.

Well, well, well. Under all those sweaters she constantly wore, Jayne was anything but plain in a swimsuit.

"My only swimsuit was all stretched out. I had this from a product placement deal last summer, and I threw it in my bag at the last minute when I remembered Wildwood Lodge had a Jacuzzi."

"No excuses required, Jayne."

"What is that quirk of a smile on your lips?" She extended a long leg downward and slipped into the steaming water beside me. For all their hurry, the others hadn't beat Jayne or me to the hot tub. And bless them for it. I had the feast of watching Jayne's approach all to myself—sans Calder the Clunker.

"I know you're thinking something, Ben. Spill it."

"Just that you could do product placement on your show for other things besides toilet brush wreaths."

"Like self-tanner? I'm probably as pale as a ghost."

"Like bikinis." And she'd sell ten million. The company would raise her to demigoddess status, just like I was doing now.

"Ben!" She pushed a handful of water at me, splashing my chest.

Then, her eyes fell on my chest—and remained there. I don't go around shirtless all that often, so I felt a hint of self-consciousness, until I saw how appreciative she was of my upper-body physique. Ah, if all the girls in college in the psych department who back in the day thought I was a sunken-chested geekface could see me now. When I'd gotten the TV spot, O'Keefe had recommended I try to buff up.

I'd tried. And succeeded.

"I had fun skating with you," Jayne said, floating a hint closer. Her leg brushed mine.

"I had a good time talking with you," I countered. And I meant it. Even the moment when I'd been slammed with the memory of my Big Mistake and its consequences, which was why I was at Wildwood Lodge in the first place. "You make me want to tell you things." In fact, I'd almost spilled my guts to her about the car accident that took

Grandma and Grandpa that I'd been the cause of. "What is it about you?"

"My charm?" She flashed me a flirtatious smile and flipped her hair, the ends of which were wet—again. Twice in one day, treat for me. "My empathetic, open-hearted ways?"

Actually, that, probably. Her open-hearted ways had me panting for more and more connection with her.

"When I was in my *Listening for Counselors* class at Dartmouth," I said, "we talked about things listeners can do to help others open up to them." Funny, Jayne had managed to embody pretty much every single one of them on the shore of the skating pond earlier. "You're a natural at all of them."

She'd listened without pushing, and she'd pulled back on the questions when she'd seen how I was feeling too vulnerable—read my body language cues like they were her native tongue.

Which thought, naturally, sent my eyes searching for her mouth.

The tiniest drop of water rested in the center of her lower lip.

That shouldn't stay there. I should kiss that off.

I clasped her elbow and floated her nearer. In the process, I pretty much forgot everything else, so captured I was by the feel of her skin against mine. I pulled her closer, closer. I could kiss this woman. She felt so right in my embrace. I ran my other hand across her waist, up her spine ...

"Hey, people. We're here!" Seneca wore a fuzzy red bathrobe and clomped in nurse's clogs across the wood slats of the deck.

Jayne floated out of my arms, leaving them emptier than they'd ever felt.

"You two warming up after your bone-chilling time on the pond?" She dumped her robe, revealed her black one-piece swim tank that looked competition-ready, and jumped into the water beside us. "Looks pretty warm in here. Calder should be along soon. He said he didn't need help limping down here. I think he was texting some family."

The last thing I cared about at this moment was who Calder the

Clunkhead was texting.

"How's his ankle?" Jayne floated in front of one of the jets. It made her hair floof up in the water now and then.

I slipped back to my spot on the ledge, the water not nearly as hot as my blood.

Chapter 12

Jayne

"He found it!" Seneca flipped a wreath-shaped pancake and beamed as I entered the kitchen. "Ben Bellamy is amazing, and I'm not just talking about those broad shoulders or that hunky walk of his. Guy has a strut on him, right?"

And a great smile. And a lot of other qualities.

"What did he find?" I asked, popping a silver-dollar-size blueberry pancake in my mouth.

Ben's smile had decorated all my dreams last night. So had the memory of his touch. Mmm. That hot tub had been dangerously warm—in more ways than one.

"A horse-drawn sleigh."

What! First the chainsaw, then the skates, and now this? "Where?"

The back door of the lodge shut, and in came Ben, stomping his boots. "I hope you don't mind that I took the initiative and rounded up a sleigh ride for us."

"But, where?" I'd shaken down every contact in my phone—and in my producer Gilda's, and in my high school friends Mallory and

81

Emily's phones, and anyone else I could hit up—but to no avail. "Another coach friend?"

He shook his head. "Actually, I just walked down the lane to the next cabin and asked. They had one in their shed—and a horse. They're willing to give us a ride. It's a grandfatherly fellow, and he said he's wanting to exercise his horse, but that we need to be ready to go by ten."

Ten! That was in an hour. "We'll be ready."

A few minutes before ten, we waited, all bundled up, in front of the Wildwood Lodge.

"I'll hold that." Calder took the blanket from Seneca's arms. "This is your wish, right? A sleigh ride. Can I ask why? Because of the historic song?"

"It's a Thanksgiving song more than a Christmas song," Seneca said. "But, yeah. I mean, Jayne asked what would make it a perfect Christmas, and this is the first thing I thought of. It's always been something I wanted to do—with cool people I enjoy."

The last phrase seemed tacked on, as if she meant to say something else—*with someone I love.*

My gaze darted to Ben. Again. *Why, when I'm supposed to be falling for Calder?*

But I wasn't. As great as Calder was, and as kind and thoughtful— we just weren't connecting. Meanwhile, all I could feel when Ben came near was electrical currents running from him into every part of me.

Basically, he'd nearly electrocuted me in the hot tub last night.

The sleigh pulled up.

"Wow. It's classic." My breath whooshed out. Red, carved wood with scrollwork, and a tufted leather seat, on beautiful shiny rails. The horse was a dapple gray with a shiny black mane and tail. "Beautiful," I said to the driver. "What's his name?"

Ben patted the horse's neck. It whinnied and nickered.

"Dalmatian." The driver introduced himself to each of us, shaking our hands. "I'm Charlie Case. Thanks for letting me do this. I used to take people on rides every winter, but when the family moved out and Wildwood Lodge turned into a vacation home, I lost that personal connection. This means a lot to me. Thanks, Ben." He gave a manly chin-jut in Ben's direction. "And it's good to meet you in person. My wife and I watch your show every night."

"We all appreciate you for making this experience possible." Ben stepped back. "Who is going first?"

The sleigh couldn't fit six, only four.

"Me, please?" Seneca stepped inside, excited. "Is it all right if we sing as we go?"

"We love to sing." Lester and Chieko climbed in, facing backward.

Who would join them? Should I? I should, but something made me hang back. *I want some time alone with Ben.*

For a long moment, Calder and Ben stared at each other, neither moving a muscle.

"It's all right. We can just go with three and three," Seneca offered.

"No, I'll go." Calder climbed in beside Seneca. "In honor of one of the best holiday songs. Mr. Case, do you think you could literally take Seneca here over a river and through some woods?"

"I'd love to."

Dalmatian whinnied again, stamped a hoof, and the sleigh took off.

As it left, Ben placed a hand on the small of my back. "They grow up so fast."

Goofball. "How long will the ride be, do you think?"

"At least an hour, Mr. Case told me. He has a route he likes to take." He took my hand and led me up the porch steps, back into the cabin.

Heat radiated off the fireplace. We removed our jackets. He looked so good in his muscle-hugging Henley shirt.

"I guess we have an hour alone." *Just like I'd wished for. But ... now what? All I want to do is kiss him. But he's Ben Bellamy. He's so out of my league.*

Ben Bellamy was a celebrity known far and wide for his insight and charm and kindness. Case in point, his charisma had netted our group a sleigh ride this morning—from a couple who watched his show nightly.

Who was I? Nobody. A quirky morning show host with a distant crush on him.

"Would you"— Ben looked at the tree, at the fireplace's mellow blaze, and then back at me—"like to dance?"

My breath caught. "Here? Now?"

"In front of the fire, near the tree. I'll put on some music."

Chapter 13

Ben

I t was probably strange to ask Jayne to dance at this time of day, but I wasn't going to let this chance get past me.

I put on the music. *The* music.

"Bing Crosby?" she asked.

"Mmm," I said as der Bingster crooned through the speakers.

I took Jayne firmly in my arms, pressing the center of her back to bring her to me. My other hand clasped hers, a cool fit. I slipped my hand across her spine and the softness of her cashmere sweater. The scents of the fire and the tree's balsam filled the air.

"You're a good dancer," I hummed into her ear. Jayne was liquid in my arms. "Have you studied?"

"Never." She met my eyes. "I think dancing with you makes me good at it."

She responded to my every lead. The song filtered in and out of my brain. Floral and citrus notes from her perfume clouded out any worries, any caution.

"May I have this dance, too?" I asked when the song ended. "White Christmas" played again, this time a low, sultry version sung by someone other than Bing Crosby, but it created an even mellower mood.

Jayne melted in my arms again. I turned her softly to the rhythm.

The fire popped. I held her closer, and she became even more supple against me.

The moment that I'd fantasized about all my life was right here, with Jayne. I was dancing with the perfect girl, to the perfect song, in the perfect setting.

"May your days be merry and bright," I hum-sang into her ear. My singing skills were lacking, but she snuggled even closer, and I couldn't hold back any longer.

Heaven.

I was falling for Jayne. Falling in *love* with Jayne. I closed my eyes and just lived the perfect moment.

"How are you, Ben?" she asked, low and alluring.

"Me? I'm dancing with the most incredible woman to my grandparents' favorite Christmas song in front of a fire and a decorated tree." My blood surged. This was it—my best Christmas. My perfect Christmas. She'd given it to me. "I'm in heaven."

"Oh?" Jayne tilted her face upward, and her lips parted in invitation.

My lips brushed hers briefly. She let out a soft sigh. I pressed a little more, with all the restraint I could muster but I was too hungry for this moment to leave it at that for more than a couple of beats of my thrumming heart. She'd strung me along for a million years, ratcheting up my desire for her with every toss of her hair, every dip of her toe in the Jacuzzi, every appearance in front of me in nothing but a bath towel. Not to mention every conversation we'd had where she'd seen into my very soul, and brought me out of my hiding places.

The pressure of her full lips was like a European racetrack's starting gun, all engines blasting at once. Jayne's luscious kiss was winning every marathon, smashing every tennis volley, making every hit on the first pitch.

I luxuriated in the kiss, the velvet stroke of her lips against mine, the feel of her hands on the ridges of my back. She kissed like she lived—free and wild and unexpected, every inch of her curvaceous form melding against my torso. She kissed me until I was ready to move to the next base, and the next, and until we were sliding into home.

Whoo. Hang on, cowboy. Not a good idea to let my thoughts spiral quite so far in that direction. I broke the kiss. She was breathing quickly.

"That was some kiss, Jayne. I'm more impressed by you every day."

"By me?" Jayne's eyes widened. "Everything I planned for this week has been a mess. I'm a mess."

"You're lovely. Everyone is comfortable here. They're having a perfect Christmas. Although, none as perfect as mine." I dipped my head and took her mouth again, a shot from the three-point line and *whoosh!* Nothing but net. Her kiss was every tournament. She made me every champion.

"Ben," she breathed, running a soft hand up my chest. It roved up into my hair. "You could bottle that kiss of yours and make millions."

"I'd only sell it to one customer." I kissed her once more, but when it got too heated again—faster this time—I scolded myself and scaled back. This was not a girl I should move too quickly with. *With her, I want it to last.*

"I like kissing you in front of the Christmas tree," I said.

"A tree *without* tacky decorations." A wry smile lifted one side of her mouth. "I know you saw my boxes and were horrified. It's not like you kept it a secret."

"About that. Why the tacky stuff? Nothing about you personally seems tacky."

"I guess I just never had a chance to learn what's *not* tacky." She led me to the couch, where we sat down even closer than we had during the movie.

Fine with me. I wrapped her in my arms and clung tightly to her.

"So, what about you, Jayne? Why aren't we doing any of your childhood favorites as activities up here in the mountains?"

"I told you."

"That your parents kind of petered out on Christmas celebrations by the time you came along? Sure, but you don't mean there was *nothing* they did to 'make the season bright.'"

One shoulder lifted and dropped. "I'm by far the caboose of the family. My next older sister—and there are four older kids in the family—is fifteen years older than I am. Mom and Dad had shifted gears into *service holidays*. Like I said the other night, I spent most of my Christmas breaks in places like impoverished Caribbean islands doing post-hurricane season cleanup."

I honed in on one word. "Most?"

"I mean, there was one year, when I was sixteen, that I begged to stay with relatives while they went jetting off. I spent some of the holiday with friends up at a mountain cabin like this. Well, a fraction of this size." She bit her lip and looked into the fireplace, as if there was something else she wasn't telling me about that time. "So, yeah. I honestly don't have any solid family traditions to hark back to. I'm just loving everything everyone else is bringing to the table—and trying to recreate it to the best of my TV-watching-to-learn-about-Christmas abilities. Which—you've seen—are meager."

"You're doing fine." Great, even. But there was more she wasn't telling me. "Did they do other things, like birthdays?"

"Here and there. It depended on their schedules."

"But you're pretty dedicated to doing things to the hilt."

"Overcompensation. Pure and simple." She smiled as if this was a self-deprecating joke, but it seemed like there was truth in the dark humor of her words. "I probably tend toward the overly fancy just to balance things out from what I missed early on."

It slapped me, like a textbook example from my schooling. The woman hadn't been nurtured. "You deserved better." My voice came out hoarse, gravelly.

Jayne met my gaze. She searched mine as if to gauge my sincerity, as if she thought I couldn't mean what I'd said. After a moment, she sat back. "There's another reason I'm hosting this event. It'd be disingenuous to pretend I'm simply inventing my lost childhood or out of altruism for singletons in my same state of alone-for-the-holidays."

"Oh?" The fireplace crackled, and a log settled lower, sending up sparks. "What kind of ulterior motive could there be for giving people a perfect Christmas?" People like me, who had been so blocked against it for ages—people who desperately needed the catharsis of Christmas in order to move on in life.

I ache to tell her about why I've needed it.

"There's a career aspect to it." Jayne leaned her head against my chest. "The other two guests I mentioned but who haven't come yet?"

"Yeah. You said they're in TV, too." I'd almost forgotten about them. "There are still two empty bedrooms."

"They are coming to evaluate whether I'd be a good fit for their national show. A sort of pre-job-interview interview." She tensed against me, as if nervous, as if this chance was everything to her.

"You're aiming for a national market? That's great!" So great. I hugged her tighter to show how happy I was. "So, so great." I kissed her forehead, her temple, her cheek, to show how happy I was for her.

She kissed me sumptuously.

"I believe in you, Jayne." So much. She deserved the recognition, I thought through a muddled fog of kissing. Jayne deserved everything wonderful. She was the coolest, most unexpected, exciting person I'd met.

And she got me through my block. I'd done it.

I'd done it not so much for Grandma, it turned out, as for myself.

Grandma and Grandpa—it's finished. Can I move on now? Will you forgive me?

I kissed Jayne again and didn't listen for an answer.

Chapter 14

Jayne

I, Jayne Renwick, was kissing Ben Bellamy. A lot. We were full-on making out. And it was the most delicious morning of my entire life, times ten.

He kissed me again and again in the soft glow of the tree's lights, his hand pressing into my lower back, his other hand fingering my hair. I almost couldn't breathe normal air. All I could breathe was Ben.

I was falling. *Timberrr.* Falling for his kiss, but more for his good heart, his kind protectiveness over me, and his love for family and all things good. Throw in his problem-solving mind and his belief in me, and Ben Bellamy was all I'd ever dreamed of and so much more.

My life had just turned on its side—and I never wanted it to turn back. Gilda would never believe it. I couldn't believe it myself. The best, most gorgeous, brightest, most desirable man in my whole world *wanted me.*

Boy, did he want me. It was evident in his every movement.

Soon, we would have to dial down our intensity, but the emotion was still sizzling and zapping like a live wire for now.

Ben's eyes were even deeper blue in the firelight. "You, Jayne, are amazing," he whispered between kisses.

No one had ever called me amazing before. No one had ever *believed* in me before. And Ben had said it—verbatim. Those words had lit my soul on fire for him.

Ben came for my kiss again and again, taking it like every kiss now and in the future belonged to him. Soon, they might.

I forgive myself for the mistake about Calder being my wish come true. What a charming side-story to discovering the pure magic of Ben Bellamy in my life.

"You're ... wow," I breathed between his expert assaults. "You might have a master's degree in psychology, but you've got a doctorate in kissing me."

"It's all I want to do."

"Same." And then, I sobered some.

Kissing Ben Bellamy is like a soufflé—airy, light, and easy to deflate.

"What is it?" Ben slowed his roll. "You all right?"

His kiss was paradise and purgatory rolled into one bright flash.

"No, it's just ..." That he was too good for me—and, at the same time, that my snowfall wish had something else in store for me. "I never want to stop kissing you."

But now that he'd kissed me, he'd forget me instantly, turn his attention back to the proverbial game, just like every other guy I'd kissed.

And I'll be alone again. And it will seem a million times lonelier because I've known him and how this feels physically and spiritually.

"Jayne—?"

"Hey, guys?" Seneca threw the front door wide. "That was the single greatest hour of my holiday life. Thank you!" She came in and threw herself onto the recliner.

"Is it our turn now?" I pulled out of Ben's arms. "Is Mr. Case waiting?"

"Oh, yeah. Sorry about that. His horse needed some kind of care all of a sudden. It cut our ride a little short. He apologized. If you want to go by later, you can try to reschedule with him, he said."

Calder, Lester, and Chieko came in, stomping their boots.

Ben looked at me with a hint of regret. Our moment was over.

"Who wants to make cookies?" Seneca asked. "You said you have a recipe, Ben Bellamy? Man who has everything?"

He did have everything. He might even have me. Whether I could withstand the coming rejection or not.

Chapter 15

Ben

"I can't get enough of these cookies." Seneca took another big bite. "They're amazing. The best recipe ever. My ex loved sugar cookies."

"Thanks," I managed. My brain had barely conjured up the recipe—since Jayne hadn't brought one—from Grandma, since it was still in the soup of memories of this morning's amazing kiss.

Jayne. *Jayne, Jayne, Jayne.* Jayne on ice. Jayne on a ladder. Jayne playing a piano duet. Jayne laughing about pasta.

Jayne—now covered with frosting and flour. She was a blooming mess—normally my least-favorite thing.

But I can't resist her. We're north and south ends of two supercharged magnets. I can't pull away. I couldn't if I wanted to. And no, I don't want to. I want that kiss every moment I breathe. I didn't get a chance to ask why she pulled away. I'll corner her later to ask. Maybe in the hallway. Maybe back in the Jacuzzi ...

Everyone was gathered around the kitchen island wearing various shades of sugar cookie dough and frosting on their midsections.

Jayne, however, had managed to get it everywhere.

She glanced down at her sweater. "I'm a mess. The cookies are covering me scalp to ankles."

"You wear it well," Seneca said.

No kidding. I wouldn't mind helping her get that frosting off.

"I haven't baked in years. And I don't think I've decorated a cookie since I was a little girl." Chieko held up her decorated snowman cookie. "I'm not good at this, but it's so fun. It feels like Christmas."

"I'd take a picture, but my hands might encrust the phone." Jayne looked helpless and so cute. "Anyone?"

Lester took photos, including some selfies—which he managed to include Chieko in. Good for him.

The decorating continued.

"Who needs the piping gun?" Jayne held it up to share, now that she'd drawn a thin line around the edges of her Christmas ornament cookie, making a pattern like Charlie Brown's t-shirt across the middle. "Who's up next?"

Seneca reached for it, and Jayne bumped me with her hip as she passed it to her. Accident, or …? I wanted it to be on purpose.

"Can I switch it out for the star tip?" Seneca replaced the narrow circle with a different tip in the frosting bag. "This recipe is to die for, Ben. Give your grandma my compliments."

"I will, when I see her." *After I die.* "She loved to bake at Christmastime."

"Who doesn't?" asked Lester with a full mouth.

"My family," said Calder and Jayne at the same time. They caught each other's glances, and smiled, laughing.

"Mine would rather hang drywall," Calder continued.

"Mine would rather save the world."

I died a little inside. Or—more like I wished Calder would die a little inside. And outside. Why was he still here, anyway? He should go. The dude needed to abandon ship. Every time I made progress with Jayne, he stood there like a referee's flag, halting my drive down the field toward the goal line.

Well, if Calder only knew I'd already reached a first down with her, he might back off. She was still wearing a little glow from our steamy make-out.

"Cookie-decorating came into vogue during Victorian times." Calder seemingly couldn't resist the history factoids. Granted, the guy knew a lot. But did he have to prove it over and over? Please.

The women were eating it up. Ugh. I was trying not to gag on it.

"Let's line up all the cookies we have finished." Seneca pulled out a tray. "Just to admire our work."

One by one, everyone added their decorated cookies to a holiday-themed tray. Ornaments, Christmas trees, Santas, candy canes—all the shapes and colors.

Grandma would have loved this moment. I loved this moment. It was perfect.

"Hey, Jayne and Ben, I'm so sorry you missed the sleigh ride." Seneca handed Lester the frosting-piping bag. "It was a dream come true for me. Do you know, we did go over a river and through some woods—to Mr. Case's grandmother's cabin deep in the woods? If the horse hadn't gotten spooked, you could have had the same experience. I'm so sorry."

Jayne met my eyes. "Actually, Ben and I still had a good time."

Hark—the herald angels, yes, we did have a good time.

"Thanks, Ben, for arranging that." Seneca came over and pecked me on the cheek. "You're this big celebrity, but you've got a heart of gold. It's pretty cool to find out that you're just as thoughtful in real life as you appear on TV."

"Ha." I couldn't hold that back. "Not everyone would say that."

Jayne elbowed me, getting flour on my Henley shirt. "There are some people at the news station who call him Glacier Man."

Glacier Man! "Hey, I thought it was Sports Brain. Glacier Man."

"You could be friendlier."

"Yeah, yeah." I could be friendlier at work, but what people didn't understand was how tricky it was to walk the line Grandpa had laid down for me—to be the perfect sports guru. Meanwhile, I only had my psychology degrees as my cred. "But cut a guy some slack who knows how to rustle up a horse-drawn sleigh."

"Fine. You can officially be done with the Glacier Man title. But you will always be Sports Brain."

"So, you're saying you like me for my brain," I said—before remembering that everyone was listening while I flirted. Great.

"That's good." Seneca placed a completed cookie on the counter. "Since the rest of us like you for your body."

When everyone laughed, even Calder, I exhaled. The flirt was just a joke to them.

I gazed at Jayne, thinking about all she'd told me.

All Jayne's life she'd been practicing her mask of serenity—when I would wager she had a variety of storms going on inside. Things hadn't been easy for her, and she'd seemed to develop a carefree vibe, easy-come, easy-go. Sure, that made sense as a survival tactic. Don't get too attached to anything because it might not pan out. Even family might not be reliable. She'd honed her attitude carefully over time, and even created a persona for herself to keep herself going when things were confusing or dark.

But she was light—she could light my night sky with her fireworks anytime.

"You all right, man?" Calder asked. "You look like you're having an aneurism."

Okay, I probably had a dumb look on my face.

Now, I had another mission: kiss this woman again as soon as possible. How could I get her away from Calder? How could I get her alone again?

"Excuse me." Calder pulled the chiming phone from his pocket and left the room.

Well, well, well. It seemed the universe agreed with my plans and had gotten rid of him.

I positioned myself next to Jayne at the counter where Calder had stood. "Nice Charlie Brown t-shirt."

"You recognize it?" Jayne held it up beside her cheek. "I'm a huge Peanuts fan."

"Linus Van Pelt is my spirit animal. So philosophical, such a deep thinker." When I grew up eventually, I wanted to be Linus.

"You know that doesn't make sense, right? He's not an animal." Jayne took a bite of her Charlie Brown cookie. "Mm. This is good. Really good. It is flaky but moist. It's got exactly the right amount of vanilla, too. It's like sweet ambrosia, the food of the gods."

I took my first bite of a cookie. The way Jayne described it, how could I not? Or while watching her lips as she chewed.

"Mmm," I said, but meanwhile, I really might have had an aneurism. The nostalgic recipe shot me through a time machine into Grandma's kitchen when I was a boy. Barely sweet, crumbly but moist, with the frosting providing most of the sugariness. Like Grandma's love on a plate.

You can't see me, but you can still sense me. We still love you, even if we're gone. The voice might have been real. Or not.

"How is it to you?" she asked.

"Perfect." I managed to keep the catch out of my voice.

Indeed, this was another truly perfect Christmas moment. Wildwood Lodge had brought it about. The tingling I'd felt when I arrived shimmered all around me.

No, this hadn't been the lodge. It'd been Jayne doing all this for me. For all of us.

"I can't believe you had that recipe memorized, right down to the half-teaspoons. Who memorizes sugar cookie recipes? I mean, salsa or how much water to add to pancake mix, but the whole cookie recipe? Impressive."

"You think I'm impressive, eh?" I said low enough for only her to hear—but she might not have anyway, since Calder reentered the room at that moment.

"What's wrong?" she asked, her voice tender.

Too tender. I could've punched the guy.

"Welp." Calder shrugged. "That's that, I guess."

"What's what?" Seneca asked. She ran to his side, anxious and caring. My favorite psychology professor would have labeled her personality an archetype of *the helper*. "You're going home? Because holidays are about family, and your family needs you, and that's where you belong?"

Seemed *someone* had been doing some persuasive reasoning on the sly. I could've bought Seneca a lifetime supply of band-aids for it!

"You were right, Seneca. I'm needed, and wanted, at home." Calder turned to Jayne, took her by both hands. "Thanks for helping me forget—and to remember. I'm not totally *there* yet—after last year—but it helped, and I'm okay with going back now. Thanks." He graze-kissed her cheek.

"But, Calder." Jayne's face clouded. "You didn't get to read us Dickens by the fire."

Yes, he did. He hit us with a few quotes the other night, and we watched the whole movie.

"What we read was enough." He patted her upper arms and turned to me. "Best wishes to you." Was that look jealousy or a concession?

No matter. He was touching her. I boiled over—silently.

But he was leaving.

All to my benefit. "Safe travels, man." *Chump.*

"I'll try to catch your show sometime, Ben. Thanks for the meals, Seneca. Nice to meet you Chieko and Lester." Calder hoisted his already-packed backpack onto his shoulder. "You all have a Merry Christmas, okay?"

And then he was gone.

"No Dickens tonight." Lester shook his head. "Seneca? Didn't you want to watch *Die Hard?* I'll stoke the fire so it will be the perfect level after dinner."

"I'll help!" Chieko followed him—tiptoe running, and she clasped his hand.

98

Lester and Chieko were moving things fast. I thought maybe I should consider putting on speed with Jayne. Not just physical. Sure, I wanted the physical but all the rest, too—the openness, the unpredictability, that undeniable emotional connection that I'd only ever felt with Jayne Renwick.

I wanted Jayne's shimmering fairy dust sprinkled all over me.

We spent the evening with Christmas gunfire and justice.

When the movie ended, everyone else went off to bed, but I sat with Jayne near the dying embers in the hearth. She was asleep on my shoulder.

Perfect? Almost—since we weren't kissing.

But, then, Jayne's eyes flew open. They held alarm, not peace.

"What's wrong?"

"Calder's gone. And it's all my fault."

What? My muscles tensed, and I scooted out from beneath her weight. She sat up straight, too, rubbing the side of her head.

"What are you talking about, Jayne?"

Jayne blinked a dozen times, as if returning from a different reality. "I'm sorry. That was—that was a weird dream."

Hmm. But she'd been dreaming about Calder. And guilt had colored it.

"It's probably time to head up to bed." I helped her to her feet and sent her up the stairs, but I stayed in the living room watching the embers—embers that glowed but would soon fade out.

Chapter 16

Jayne

Calder was gone. *Gone.* And it was my fault.

My dream had been so realistic that I'd awakened from it with horror, even to the point of shouting my panic aloud to Ben. Now, I couldn't sleep again, and the dream's truths distilled on me, dews of understanding and insight.

I flopped on my bed and texted Gilda all about it.

Moments later, she responded.

But you didn't wish on the snow for a history teacher with dark hair. You wished for a hot English teacher who looked like Mr. Deloitte.

Whoa. That wasn't wrong.

But still, I told her, I could have done better with the incredible opportunity that the first-snowfall wish had provided me. I could have spent my formative years preparing for Calder's advent in my life—by reading all the books in the library, by watching all the historical documentaries and not just the ones forced on me by Mallory, and by studying articles on little-known history facts online.

I could have made it work. I wasted my preparation time! I didn't read any history books. I squandered my one shot with him.

What was that quote from Dickens that Calder had slapped us with the first night we were all together around the fire? Something about regret? I did an internet search and found it.

No space of regret can make amends for one life's opportunity misused.

Precisely.

I wallowed for a while, curling into a crunched ball. The dark of night gave me no clarity.

Finally, Gilda's response appeared.

I found your high school yearbook online. Don't think I'm stalking. I just wanted to see what your hunky Mr. Deloitte looked like. Mmm. Check him out.

A photo attachment appeared as the next text, and my stomach flipped.

The resemblance is pretty uncanny, eh? she added. There followed a bunch of those annoying laugh-cry emojis. **You've either got Ben Bellamy <u>pre</u>-incarnated, or you've got some distant relative relationship going on.**

Uncanny was right. So alike! Especially around the eyes. Ooh, and the bow of his upper lip. And the set of his jaw. And the coloring, so fair and irresistible. I did love a blond guy, and those piercing blues. Mmm.

The similarities were definitely strong. The way Mr. Deloitte had talked with so much authority and compassion. The insights. The way he filled up my belly when he entered the room.

All just like Ben Bellamy.

My brain filled with those exclamation-point-question-mark duos. Me? Had I actually snowfall-wished *Ben Bellamy* into my life?

And if so, how long until he dumped me?

My head hurt. I went back to sleep. Maybe sleep would bring me clarity between these two opposing ideas.

101

Chapter 17

Ben

The next morning, no sign of Jayne. None at lunch, either. I stood on the deck of Wildwood Lodge, my breath steaming, a visible sign of my frustration.

I'd kissed her. She'd fallen asleep in my arms—after which she'd only talked about Calder Kimball.

What was with that? Honestly, while it hurt on a deep level, it confused my ego. Women threw themselves at me. They offered to have my babies. They followed me in the hardware store, giggling.

And yet Jayne Renwick was obsessed with a boring school teacher? Nice enough guy, but not for Jayne!

I had to get to the bottom of it—because her kiss had told me a whole different story. On a molecular level, the woman wanted me. Not him.

"You look troubled." Lester joined me on the front porch, handing me a cup of hot cider.

"I'm all right." The cider was fruity and spiced. It warmed all the way down.

Chieko's piano playing filled the air, a rendition of one of

Tchaikovsky's *Nutcracker Suite* songs—the one where the clowns dance? Grandma would've been disappointed in me for forgetting.

Lester looked over his shoulder. "Is there anything that girl of mine can't do?" Lester sipped from his mug. "Chieko Parsons. She skates, she plays the piano, she's a teacher with a teaching heart. I … I am just so glad I signed up for this lodge retreat."

"That's great, man." I rubbed my face. Everything in the last twelve hours had me off my game.

"You got something in your eye?" Lester gave me an amused look.

"Maybe." Confusion.

"Something in your eye like a girl with light brown hair who looks like a swimsuit model in a bikini? Because you should go after that. Do not miss your target."

"Thanks." Jayne did have the bikini body of every man's dreams. But she had a lot more attractions beyond the physical. Most attractive of all, she was helping me process the deepest and oldest wounds of my heart.

"Put her in your sights and pull that trigger." Gun metaphors made sense for a military guy. "Quit stalling."

"Do you think there was anything between her and Calder?"

"Mutual respect?" Lester shrugged. "What do *you* have to worry about? I've seen how she looks at you, like she wants to have you for dinner *and* dessert."

She did? "I haven't seen her today, have you?"

"She went into town. Something about tape for wrapping gifts."

Of course Jayne would have forgotten something as vital as Scotch tape. "Were we supposed to bring gifts?"

"Jayne said she brought some for everyone. Not a big gift at all, she said, but she claimed it's not Christmas without presents." Lester drained his mug. "I'm thinking about going into town myself. Getting something really significant for Chieko."

"Significant?" I took the bait.

"When you know, you know." He smiled. "Soldiers tend to make bold moves when it comes to committing to women. We just don't know what the next deployment will bring."

He was going ring-shopping? "But you met her this week."

"This won't sound like a soldier talking, but my soul has known hers forever."

Good night! The guy was going to propose! Wildwood Lodge's spell perhaps. Or was it the forced proximity of those reality shows? Either way, Lester was drinking the Kool-aid.

"Good for you," I said. *I wish I knew like Lester knows.* I mean, I was starting to know. Our kissing had told me almost as many things as our conversations, like we knew each other body and soul.

However, Jayne's sudden pulling away had me spooked.

I needed to sort this out.

Meanwhile, what could I give Jayne for a Christmas gift?

Chapter 18

Jayne

Maybe it made me a bad or inconsistent hostess, but this morning I'd had to get out of there. Wildwood Lodge had woven some kind of spooky tapestry over me that was messing with my brain.

It had made me think I was falling hard for Ben Bellamy.

Falling in love.

Sure, I'd always had it bad for the guy. Just like every woman who'd ever encountered him in real life or on screen.

But, if I *fell* for him, I was in for a world of hurt. Any second now, he'd refocus on whatever he found more interesting than me.

So, I'd left. I'd gone the forty-five minute drive into town. I'd shopped. I'd wrestled with the conundrum.

And, like a coward, I'd returned to Wildwood Lodge with no answers, no courage to break things off with Ben before he broke them off with me.

Like a loser.

Again.

"O Christmas tree, O Christmas tree." We sang carols as I placed the gifts I'd just wrapped under the tree. Chieko accompanied. It was like my faint, earliest memories of the one time we had a family Christmas. My sister had played the piano, and we all sang fun songs, placing gifts beneath the tree in heaps.

"The tree is so big, it makes the piles under the tree seem scant." I tried to fluff them out to make them look more plentiful.

"Can we open presents even though it's not Christmas Eve until tomorrow?" Seneca asked.

"Hey, Christmas presents don't get opened until Christmas Day," Ben chimed in firmly on this point. "It's tradition."

"Your tradition, maybe, but in my family, we opened them when we received them," Chieko said. "So that we could immediately thank the giver."

"I like that." Opening them all right now would be fun. Besides, we'd already spent two nights watching movies, and there should be a different activity. "Why not change it up, Ben?"

Ben looked at me warily. Ever since I'd returned this afternoon, he'd been distant.

Okay, I couldn't blame him, considering what I'd said when I woke up from that disturbing dream last night about Calder.

Ben looked pained, but he obviously manned up, making his voice sound casual. "My grandparents might turn over in their graves, but if everyone else wants to do presents tonight, all right. I'll back down."

"Yes!" Lester fist-pumped the sky. "Let's dig in!"

"One at a time!" Seneca called. "We're not five-year-olds, and this is not a free-for-all. We can at least do that."

"Thank you," Ben said, as if this dialed down his change-anxiety a full notch. "One at a time."

Everyone took turns opening the wrapped boxes of Christmas-themed pajamas I'd brought.

"How did you know my size?" Chieko asked, hugging her reindeer and jingle bells fleece to her chest. "I love these. They're so soft."

I'd asked for everyone's sizes in the original questionnaire.

"I *moose* have a kiss?" Ben held his up, a skeptical brow rising too. "When did you choose this saying for mine?"

Oh, I'd chosen them without even knowing Ben would be the Grand Poobah of kissing—before I'd even known Benson Smith was Ben Bellamy. "That's my secret," I said mysteriously, but probably coming off like a doofus.

"Sounds like you'd better grant the woman's wish." Lester chuckled evilly. "Why don't we have any mistletoe around here, anyway? There'd be an ideal excuse and location."

Ben and I hadn't needed any excuse for our kisses last night while dancing in front of the tree or getting close on the couch. Now, all I could think about when I looked at him was how his lips felt on mine. My breath caught again.

"Ahhhh!" Seneca screamed.

"Seneca!" I flew to her side, crouching near the armchair, where she had taken her *Christmas Heals Hearts* with a nurse decal pajamas out of the package. "What on earth?"

Seneca buried her face in the crook of her elbow. "It finally happened! The thing I've been wishing for!"

Her response had sounded so agonizing—like she'd received something no one would wish for.

"What do you mean?" Chieko abandoned Lester and came to Seneca's side, too. "What did you wish?"

"That Ivan would ask for me back. I told him we were through—right before Thanksgiving."

The breakup had been in her paperwork. "And? Did he message you?" Her deepest, fondest wish had come true? *Thank you, Wildwood Lodge.*

"Yes"—she gulped—"he just messaged, begging me to come back—to be there with him for Christmas Eve tomorrow. He's going to let me roast the turkey. He thawed it and everything. Even bought one of those expensive oven bags. He *apologized*. Said he loves me and is ready to move forward again." She swiped at tears and sniffled. "I love him, guys. I hate abandoning you all when you've been so great and given me so many memories and a way better Christmas than I could have dreamed otherwise." She jumped up from her chair and hugged each of us in turn. "Can you manage the cooking without me? I feel so guilty!"

"We can manage." I hugged her a second time. This was the best gift of Christmas. Love. Love for Seneca.

"We'll miss you," Ben added, "but like you said to Calder—it's best to be with loved ones."

Ten minutes later, Seneca's tail lights disappeared down the drive, and I stood alone with Ben on the porch of Wildwood Lodge. Chieko and Lester were back inside at the piano.

"There was another gift under the tree."

"Really?" I hadn't seen one. I turned to look in the window, but Ben took my elbow.

"All right, it didn't make it under the tree. Here, though." From inside his coat, he brought out a small wrapped gift. "Christmas isn't Christmas without presents."

I stared at it for a minute. "It's … for me?" Slowly, I accepted it from his hand. People on TV shook their gifts near their ears, just to make a guess.

I didn't do that. Instead, I slipped my finger under the wrapping paper's edge at the tape.

"It was the best I could find on short notice." Ben shifted his weight.

"This is from you?" I took a half-step back. "I mean, of course. Thank you." My heart flooded with something I didn't recognize. It was warm and safe and free. "Thank you, Ben."

"You haven't seen it yet. You might not like it."

The gift was from Ben Bellamy. I'd love it no matter what. "Oh, my goodness! Ben?" My eyes pricked. "It's so … perfect." Perfectly me.

The wrapping paper dropped near my feet. In my hands was a box about the size of half a loaf of bread. It sparkled pink and red. Shiny. It was just like the wreath on the front door. Its lid had a silver latch on the front. *Could it be?*

"Open it." He gave me a nod.

Trembling, I gently popped the latch. When I lifted the lid, a plinking song began to play before I could even open it up to reveal the red velvet-lined interior with tufted spaces for rings, necklaces, earrings. "You remembered?" The pricking in my eyes grew to full-on, tear-duct pouring. He'd remembered that chance mention I'd made on our first day here at Wildwood Lodge—that I'd dreamed of a music box for jewelry! My heart careened in my chest.

"The song is my favorite," he said.

It took me a moment of listening for the song to register. "'White Christmas,'" I whispered. He'd kissed me to "White Christmas." "Thank you, Ben."

Gently, he took the box from my hands and moved it to the rail of the deck. Then, he placed a hand behind my ear and leaned in. His kiss was luxuriant. Every pass of his lips over mine was music and lyrics. I wrapped my arms around his shoulders, and he pressed me to his chest.

Safe. I was safe here in Ben's arms in the rays of the setting sun.

Ben Bellamy hadn't kissed me and forgotten me when the game came on. Ben had kissed me, and then he'd found me the perfect Christmas present—something that represented my taste *and* our first kiss.

This was the best moment of my life.

He kissed me until he should stop. We stood side by side on the covered porch, our shoulders touching.

"The only thing that could make this moment more perfect is if we had a full moon." The sky was fully twilight now. He pressed his lips to my forehead, and then I leaned my head on his shoulder.

"Yeah, too cloudy." As if cued by my words, a crystal snowflake floated down through the porch's light. "Oh! It's the first snowfall!" And all my first-snowfall wishes from when I was a girl were coming true.

"Um, I hate to break it to you." Ben swept an arm to indicate the piles of snow that covered the landscape. "Snow has fallen before tonight."

"Oh, I know. But I meant the first snowfall since we've been here." Hmm, I wondered … "Maybe we can still wish on it."

"What are you talking about?"

"You mean you don't know about the first-snowfall wish?" He didn't, so I explained. "I heard this from my friend Emily, who heard it from her grandma."

"So it has to be true. Grandmas know their stuff."

I grinned at him. "I wish I'd met your grandma."

"I wish that, too." He pulled me tighter. "Tell me about this snow wishing thing."

"On the first snowfall of the year, you catch the first snowflake you see. When it hits the palm of your hand, if you can wish before it melts, your wish will come true."

"What kind of wish? Any wish?" He brushed a stray lock of hair from my forehead.

"A wish on love, of course." I laughed. "We all did. It was tradition." I told him about Emily and Mallory. "Two of the best friends a girl like me could ever have wanted. Mallory wished for a prince, and Emily wished for a hero to kiss her on a bridge."

"And you?" A merry twinkle lit his eye. "Did you wish for a Sports Brain?"

Oh—shoot. My stomach leapt into my throat. *I should have thought about where this conversation would lead.* But I couldn't back out now. "I wished for Mr. Deloitte."

"What's that? Doily-what?"

"My high school English teacher. All the girls were secretly in love with him."

Ben's arm dropped from around my shoulder, and he shoved his hand into his pocket. "A school teacher."

110

Huge sigh. "Yeah, which—um, that might have been the cause of my confusion." I had to apologize, but how could I do it without sounding like a lunatic? "At the risk of sounding like a crazy person …"

"Go on." He turned toward me. He looked surprisingly vulnerable. "Does this have to do with Calder Kimball?"

I looked at the tips of my boots. "When I first approved him as a guest for this week, I may have thought he was the granting of my wish. But I was wrong."

"You were?" Ben angled toward me, reached over and curled a finger beneath my chin, turning my face to him.

I met his eyes. "Completely wrong." I pulled out my phone and scrolled to the text Gilda had sent me with the old pic of Mr. Deloitte. "See?"

"Who is that? He looks like he could be my brother from another decade." Ben gave it back to me. "Don't tell me … the doily?"

"Ben!" I shoved his shoulders. "It's not doily. But yeah, you do look like him. And you think and talk like he did—analysis, insight, thoughtfulness."

Warming again, he took me in his arms, turning me to face him. "You're saying, Jayne"—he pressed a kiss to my temple, to a spot below my ear, to my neck—"that I'm your girlhood wish come true?"

A car's engine sounded on the road, and lights appeared in the distance. "Who could that be at this hour?"

Chapter 19

Ben

"What's that?" Jayne asked, pulling out of my embrace. A set of headlights traveled down the gravel toward the lodge. "Who could that be at this hour of the night?"

Please say it's not Calder coming back. Or Seneca.

No one could've been worse than Calder or Seneca. Bless their hearts, but they were like speed bumps in my race to win Jayne's attention.

"Wrong turn," I said, not wanting to lose this moment. "It'll take a long time for them to get here and turn around to leave, anyway. Jayne, have you been wrong about other guys before that teacher?"

She shook her head. "I've just been … waiting, I guess. I mean, I went on a few dates and learned my lesson."

"How so?"

"This will sound pathetic, but here goes. They'd kiss me and then they'd just start watching the game again. Ask me to get them a sandwich. Apparently, I'm only good for the commercials."

Good grief, they were stupid. "Your kiss, Jayne, is so much better than commercials." I went in for another kiss. She shut me down, which was also fair. "Jerks," I said. "They did not deserve you."

"I know, right?" She smiled. "How about you? You said you dated someone in television in the past, but it was bad timing?"

Marissa. "We could have been a good fit. But she wasn't willing to wait for me to work through all my issues."

The car still hadn't turned around. It approached slowly in the snow.

"You—the psychology expert—have issues?" Jayne's laugh, even when it was soft, had that winning quality.

"Had." I pushed a stray lock of hair from where it had fallen across her pretty brown eyes. "Past tense. You, Jayne, have helped me through them more than any book I've read or course I've taken. This trip has been the final key to my healing. Thank you."

"Thank me? For a final key? What do you mean?"

"Yes, Jayne. You." I kissed her now, not accepting her reticence, not wanting to break the moment with talk of Grandma and Grandpa's accident and how Jayne had helped me finally give them what I had promised.

My boldness worked.

"When you hold me," Jayne murmured, "I don't care about your ex or anyone else."

Neither did I.

A clatter on the gravel sounded, breaking our moment. The engine cut, and out of the car stepped a man whose face nearly stopped my heart.

Marty?

Chapter 20

Jayne

The man stood on the gravel—his smile glowing like it'd been hit with a black light.

Marty! He was here!

"Oh, my goodness. Ben!" I grabbed his biceps like they'd keep me steady in this moment's earthquake. "It's them! My career-maker guests."

I hailed Marty, who stepped toward us on the gravel. "Well, if it isn't the biggest celebrity to grace Wildwood Lodge since Vanderbilt himself."

Dark-haired Marty with his boy-next-door looks and DayGlo-white smile hailed me right back. "Jayne Renwick! Merry Christmas." Then he gave a hearty ho-ho-ho, as if he were Santa Claus himself.

Well, he might've ended up becoming *my* Santa Claus, depending on how this interaction tonight went. My entire Christmas list was scrolled up in this one momentous visit.

Almost all of it, I should say. I spared a glance for Ben's reaction. "You know Marty and Marissa, right?"

Ben didn't answer. His face was a stone.

From the passenger side, Marty's sister Marissa climbed out, stretching like a cat, shaking out her voluminous dark hair. "Ahh. We finally made it. Long day of skiing, and then this gorgeous cabin, all lit up like it is welcoming us with open—"

"Arms?" I supplied, but then I noticed where she was looking.

Ben crossed his arms, folding them tightly over his chest.

Marissa shrank back. "Ben? Ben Bellamy? Is that you?"

Chapter 21

Ben

O ne second, I was standing in the starlight with a soft, pliable girl, radiating heat in my arms. The next, I was shivering in the dark and staring at the last person I *ever* wanted to see, let alone tonight, the night before Christmas Eve.

"Ben?" Marissa's voice cracked in her signature way, the way that held all of America captive during her witty interviews with famous and not-so-famous guests. "Ben Bellamy? Is that you?"

I became the petrified forest.

"Hey, man." Always-grinning Marty bounded up the steps and reached for my hand. "Good to see you again, brother."

I shook it, but my arm should've broken off and landed with a stony *thunk* on the porch.

"Between you and me, Plain Jayne"—Marty turned on his signature charm, his teeth glowing so white they lit up the dark porch more than the overhanging pendant light—"I wouldn't be embracing this dude. He broke my sister's heart last Christmas. It's all we could do to get her back on the air after the new year. But she did recover. Recently. Barely."

Marissa had gripped the door handle on the car.

"Let's hope this doesn't cause her a setback," Marty whispered to Jayne so I could hear.

"Oh," was all Jayne said.

"I must say, it's good to finally meet you in real life, Jayne." Marty assessed her, his eyes roving. I mean, what guy wouldn't? "Are you making hot cocoa? I think I smell cocoa. I have a nose for cocoa. Ask anyone." He pushed his way through the front door. "I hope you have marshmallows."

None of the remaining three of us had moved a muscle.

Marissa stood rooted to the gravel driveway, her eyes on me like I was the reincarnated ghost of her Christmases past.

Jayne had stopped breathing, if my ears served me right.

And me? I was statue-worthy at this point. That childhood game— I would've won it for sure. I couldn't move, blink, draw breath.

"What's the holdup?" Marty popped his head back out the front door, nearly whacking the ugly pink and red wreath. "You'll all catch your death out there. Jayne, come on in and show me what this *perfect Christmas* event you've organized is all about. I'm dying to see what you've done for your guests. Tell me everything, so that I get an idea of your style and personality and how you've wowed everyone. I'm sensing you're just what our show needs."

Marty pulled Jayne along into the lodge, and his voice faded as they retreated into the inner workings of the place, but Jayne still hadn't said a word.

At last, Marissa released her death-grip on the car door and took a few steps toward me, snowflakes flurrying around her like so many falling cherry blossoms—the universal symbol of the fleeting nature of life.

How fitting.

"I—I never thought I'd see you in person again. In real life." She gulped visibly.

This wasn't real life. This was Wildwood Lodge. A fairy tale— apparently complete with the nightmare aspect that all fairy tales included.

Marissa came up the steps, the vapor of her breath visible in the night air. "How have you been?"

"Good." At last, my vocal cords loosed and I could speak. "You?"

"I've missed you." Her perfume wafted toward me. She hadn't

changed it. Her hairstyle was slightly shorter, but still that deep brunette color of her signature look. Her eyelashes were thicker. Everyone had thicker eyelashes lately.

Not Jayne. Hers are natural and just the right amount.

"Did you get any messages from the station managers I told about you? They all said they'd contact you. I never heard whether you accepted their offers. You'd be great in New York, Philadelphia, or even Boston." Where she worked and lived. "Ben, you have what it takes to do a national spot, you know."

I did know. "When they called, I hadn't been ready to make a move."

"Hadn't been?" Of course Marissa would latch onto the nuance of my verb tense choice. "Does that mean—perhaps—that something fundamental has changed for you recently?"

Very recently. Like in the past three or four days, and all due to Jayne—and maybe the spell of Wildwood Lodge. "It's complex."

"It's always complex, Ben. You just have to accept that fact and move forward through the complexities. Life is one big, tangled web of difficulty, and we're here in this life to navigate it. Don't allow that fact to bring you to a halt." She pulled back a half a step. "Here I go again, saying all the same things to you that didn't work for me last time." She lowered her eyes. The lashes—although too plentiful—did look pretty against her cheek.

I thawed toward her a degree. "I say it's complex because I'm in a situation that's new. Something I wasn't banking on, and I'm not quite sure where it's leading."

"With that Jayne person." Her tone hardened.

Should I own up to it? It was so new, I had barely even admitted it to myself. "Jayne Renwick." A thunderclap jolted in my heart. Saying her name so decisively—confessing to Marissa that Jayne and I were something to each other—felt earth-shattering.

I grabbed the porch railing. A voice whispered in my head something I couldn't understand.

"Ben?" Marissa raised her eyes, those lashes fringing and fluttering. "I'm not asking you for another chance."

"You're not?"

"I'm just asking whether you're ready to come to the big city yet."

That question, at least, owned a simple response. "I believe I am."

Marissa launched herself into my arms.

Chapter 22

Jayne

Our tour of the lodge was taking forever. Marty had something to say about every single room in the house, and he asked a million questions—of which he let me answer about three—regarding our activities of the past week.

"So, you're saying you went ice skating. On a frozen pond?" Before I could describe it, he launched again. "That's quaint. Not very original, but definitely … traditional. And for dinners, you ate—?"

"Linguine the first night. With marinara sauce."

Marty looked at me like I'd dropped a *bomb of boring* on him. "Pasta. For Christmas? I guess it's original. I mean, not *that* original. Pretty pedestrian. Not something we could do a big show spot on. Were there any surprise ingredients? Did you add, say, clams to the sauce?"

"I didn't cook it." Seneca hadn't said anything about clams, and I'd been too wrapped up in Calder's presence and Ben's flirtation and pheromones to take much note that night. "I could ask the woman who was doing all the cooking for us."

"*Was* cooking? Where is she now?"

"She left. Her ex called and they got back together." Talk about the mystical power of Wildwood Lodge.

Marty nodded grimly. "She left. It was too …" The word *dull* hung unspoken but hollering near his lips.

"I swear, it's been more exciting than it might seem on the surface while just talking about the details." I grabbed my phone and scrambled through it, looking for pictures from our moments. Anything that might convey just how wonderful our time had been together.

Marty ignored my frantic waving of the phone with the photo of the sugar-cookie decorating. "The most exciting thing I'm seeing is that crocheted toilet seat cover."

"Yeah?" I brightened, and I was about to tell him how I'd come into possession of such a prize when he cut me off.

"That's not actually a compliment, Jayne. Sorry. Toilet seat covers do not the stuff of televised excitement make."

"I mean—" My argument died on my lips. "There was this one moment when—" I nearly described for him my accidental exit from the shower and into Ben's arms, but fortunately my good sense kicked in and I stopped myself.

"When?"

"Never mind. I just thought …"

"You thought?" Marty heaved a big sigh. "You thought the beauty of the location would be enough? Jayne, I watched some clips of your show on WGWG. You have some killer instincts about what will draw viewers—most of the time. Where are those instincts here at Wildwood Lodge? Because all I'm seeing is traditional, traditional, traditional."

"Aren't you and Marissa traditional?"

"Sure, we are. But that's because we serve as the foils, the straight-men for the jokester people who we hire to act as our opposites on *Good Morning, USA.*" He shifted his weight, glancing at the boring Christmas tree with its boring thirty strands of lights and normal glass ornaments. "Haven't you watched us? If not, why did you even apply for us to come meet you?"

"Of course I've watched you!" Not regularly for the past few months, but everyone knew Marty and Marissa. Their brand was legendary. "I'm your biggest fan."

He lifted a doubtful brow. "And you haven't noticed how we bring our style person on set, with their outlandish suggestions, and then when they leave, we talk about what a decorating disaster those items would be in real life?"

"That's not what you do." Ever. I'd watched them religiously and never had that happened. "You're polite and fun." I took a step back, bumping into the sofa where Ben and I had recently been kissing, where I'd discovered my first ever *safe space*. I needed Ben's arms now, while my future crumbled.

"Maybe in the past. But that's been our new style for the past three months. We had a shift in our viewership—we're capturing an even younger audience with this pivot in tone. Younger audiences want snark. They want edginess. They want us to poke fun at people."

"Even your own experts? Your friends?"

"Especially them. Why do you think Alessandra left the show? She hated the revised vibe—and I can't blame her. She did end up on the receiving end all the time." He frowned, and then brightened again. "Marissa and I have watched and seen what you've been doing, and how well you've handled all the negativity that gets thrown at you daily. You're strong. You're resilient enough to handle what we'd throw at you. Behind your back, of course. As soon as you're off-stage. You'd never have to take it in the teeth."

I crumpled into a heap—at least on the inside. "I guess—I might not have been as faithful of a viewer this past three months."

"You have to be current, Jayne." Marty picked up a book that Calder had left out, thumbed through it, and set it down without seeing a word on its pages. "We're still interested in your work, despite the no-glitz situation you've created here." He glanced around at the boringness. "But, you're going to have to be ready to take some slings and arrows."

Slings and arrows! If I had Ben at my side, could I handle them—

though they be fired at me by the likes of Marty and Marissa themselves?

Ben. Marissa.

Oh, my giddy aunt. I'd left them on the porch together. The horror show with Marty had supplanted the horror show that my life had become the second Marissa set foot out of their car.

"Ben?" I jogged toward the front door and flung it wide—just in time to see Marissa launch herself into Ben's arms.

"You're really ready to come to the city? I'm impossibly happy, Ben. You've made my Christmas dream come true." She kissed his neck, his cheek, his eyebrow.

"Ben?" I squeaked. "Ben?" My voice grew inaudibly small. I slowly shut the door and stepped back.

Marty came up beside me. "Amazing! Two seconds back in each other's presence and they've already forgiven each other for last year's misunderstanding."

He gazed at my life's destruction like it was a child on a pony.

"Maybe you were right about Wildwood Lodge, Jayne." He slung an arm around my shoulders. "There could be magic here, like you said in your email. The cook you hired—she got back together with her ex, too. Isn't it great?" Marty beamed as only a man with chemically whitened veneers could beam, the sun and the moon put together. "Jayne Renwick, thank you for making my sister happy again."

"Ah."

By trading my own future happiness for Marissa's.

Yeah, you're welcome. My heart plodded to a halt somewhere near my knees, when Marty offered the words I'd longed to hear for ages.

"And just for that," he said, "I'll make sure our producers give you a serious look when you come in for your audition." They rang like a spoon against a tin cup.

"You're letting me audition?" I asked weakly. "I'm invited to Boston to try out for your show?"

"You sure are, right after the holidays. Frankly, we owe you big time." He punched my shoulder like a big brother would. "Ben is Marissa's one true love."

Then, Marty threw the door open and went outside to collect his sister—gathering both her and Ben into a group hug. "Hey!"

One true love. The lodge swayed dangerously, dumping all the decorations off the tree and breaking all the glass ornaments against the chambers of my heart.

Marty, Marissa, and Ben all hugged on, while I stood gripping the frame of the couch, the distance between them and me growing exponentially, like I was being sucked backward through a tunnel— while all the heat in the lodge was replaced by icy air from outside.

"Ben, old buddy." Marty slapped his back congenially. "I'm guessing you'll be with us for Christmas Eve tomorrow night? Back together as part of the family again? Be sure to bring your famous sugar cookies. We're all still raving about them." Marty turned and waved me goodbye. "See you again soon, Jayne."

He went out to the car, and Marty and Marissa's sped off into the night.

Ben stared at me like he'd been caught cheating.

Because he had.

Just like every man I'd ever kissed, Ben had instantly been recaptured by the game. Like always, as soon as I let my heart get involved, the man's attention waned to nothing.

This time, I'd been even more duped, because he waited until the second kiss to ruin me.

The jewelry box had been a nice feint.

I'd fallen hard for that.

Fool.

"Good night, Ben." Brave voice, but it quavered. I turned away to keep the emotion from showing. "I assume you'll be needing the kitchen in the morning for another batch of sugar cookies. Don't worry, I'll do the dishes when I get up. It's my turn."

I raced up the stairs to my Santa Rainbow Brite bedroom and shut the door. Tight.

And, of course, someone knocked on it immediately.

"Jayne?"

"Go away, Ben. I'm not talking to you right now. Besides, you have Marissa back in your life. Go to her."

"Jayne, please. It's a misunderstanding."

"You're going to New York? To Boston? You'll be with Marissa there?"

He was silent.

See? Not a misunderstanding. "Give me a little space, please." *So I won't break down in front of you.*

Footsteps descended the stairs. Good. I could wallow in peace now. The tears welled.

But then, more knocking.

"Jayne? It's me, Chieko." Her sweet little voice forced me to pull it together. "Can I talk to you?"

I peeled myself off the bedspread and trudged to the door—then pasted on a calm, happy face and opened it. "Chieko. Hey, what's up?"

"Um, I hate to be a party pooper, but ..."

"You're leaving?" Everyone was leaving before Christmas. Before Christmas Eve, even. Why not Lester and Chieko, too? "It's all right."

A grin split her face. "It's amazing. He's amazing." She clasped her hands at her heart. "We've been video-chatting with my parents, and they invited both of us out to San Francisco. They love Lester, and he sprang for tickets for both of us. They're super expensive, but he said buying his new motorcycle can wait. In fact, I think I saw him researching minivans for sale online. Oh, my gosh! It's all going so fast that I might get wind-burned as I fly through this crazy adventure at light speed, but I don't want it to slow down a bit. When you know, you know."

Wind-burned. Heart-burned. Ben-burned. "That's great, Chieko. I am so happy for both of you."

She broke into a litany of praises for Lester, his courage, his service to the country, his wisdom and his sacrifices. "It's the real deal, Jayne, and I have you to thank for it." She threw her arms around me and hugged me tighter than an octopus squeezes its prey. "Thank you. Merry Christmas!"

And she was gone.

So was Lester.

Their cars' wheels crunched on the gravel drive, and I lay on my back on the bed, staring at the ceiling, thinking about history—*thanks, Calder*—repeating itself.

The mantra rolled. Every time I'd ever kissed a man who cared about sports—I needed to broaden my definition from mere athletes to include sports psychologists—they'd immediately gone back to watching the game.

In Ben's case, the game was winning back his ex, winning a spot on national television, and leveling up his fame.

I had to hand it to him—he was winning that game, big time.

And I was losing it. A hundred percent.

Something hot trailed down the side of my temple. I touched it. Ah, a tear. Of course.

I'm not going to cry for him. No! But the ducts weren't listening, and my pillow was getting wet.

Another knock sounded on the door. This time, it could only be one person. Everyone else had left.

"Jayne?" Ben's voice came softly, imploringly, through the door. "Can we talk?"

Um, no? Heck, no? "Hey, it's pretty exciting about your job offer in the city. You should take it. I think you're ready."

"You do?" His voice was less confident than usual.

"Totally. You've worked for it. You deserve it. Go get 'em, tiger." The gods must have been watching over me, because my voice didn't crack through any of those cheers.

"Can you just open the door?"

If he saw my tear-stained temples, he'd know. I couldn't let him.

"Please, Jayne? I—"

"I'm not decent." Sort of a lie. "Look, Ben." I stood up anyway and walked to the door, resting my forehead against it. It was the closest I'd ever be to him again, once he left this place and moved on with his life. I had to at least touch him vicariously through the wood panels.

"Jayne, it's important."

"Of course it is! It's your whole life! And you've cleared up everything leading up to it, and you're ready to move ahead. By the way, you did give every single person who came here a perfect Christmas." Even Marissa. "Even me." Almost perfect, until the end. "Mission accomplished. Thank you."

"This is how you're saying goodbye?" His voice was low, soft— possibly a little hurt.

"No, I'll add this: Merry Christmas, Ben." And I went to my bed and put my head under the pillow so he couldn't hear my sobs. "It was perfect," I said loudly, albeit through the muffle of the pillow. *Almost perfect.*

After everything, it turned out I would be spending Christmas Eve and Christmas at Wildwood Lodge alone.

Chapter 23

Ben

"Jayne, please," I begged. "Marissa isn't part of it."

She wasn't listening anymore. Something came through the door, like muffled crying.

Why? What had happened?

Jayne had been so peppy and excited for me a second ago! But then, she'd given me my walking papers. And before that, she'd accused me of returning to Marissa.

I couldn't lie to Jayne and tell her Marissa wouldn't meet me in New York. She would. She was my contact, but … ugh.

Worse, she'd acted all cheery about dumping me. Like I'd been a phase, a passing fancy. Like anything beyond the confines of Wildwood Lodge had never crossed her mind.

Easy come, easy go. That had seemed to be her life's philosophy.

Apparently, it applied to her relationship with me, as well.

It hollowed me out. I wandered through Wildwood Lodge like a zombie, collecting Grandma's Christmas decorations and loading them into the boxes, and then putting the boxes into the back of my truck. Lester and Chieko had left, and only Jayne and I remained. Jayne wouldn't want to see Grandma's nativity scene and her antique glass globe ornaments if she didn't want to see me.

It took a while, but I emptied the place of all vestiges of myself.

I walked the last box of Grandma's perfect Christmas items out to my truck. My luggage I slipped into the cab. A chill grabbed at my throat.

My insides were a gutted house. A crushed Pepsi can. A document sent through the shredder. A missed field-goal kick at the end of the fourth quarter with the team down by one.

I went upstairs one last time, a last minute end-run. It was past midnight now, and I shouldn't bother her. She was probably asleep, but I couldn't leave things as they'd been an hour ago.

"Jayne?" I whispered through the door. "If you're sure you don't want me, I can understand. These interviews for the New York sports job—they're something I've been waiting a long time to do, and I can't see myself ignoring the chance, no matter who facilitated them." Marissa had done it for me, and I did owe her at least the courtesy of responding to the offers of interviews.

No response.

"Grandma always pestered me about choosing to miss big opportunities." If Jayne couldn't handle that, I—well, I didn't know what could be done about it.

Why was she rejecting me so soundly? I'd thought we had something!

"Don't you see what a huge break this could be?" I pleaded. "I've been putting it off for so long—until I'd finally crossed *perfect Christmas* off my list in my grandparents honor." Jayne was the reason I'm at a place where I can be open to growth in my career. Finally. "I've spent all this time making reparations. I'm finally there."

The door cracked open, revealing Jayne's beautiful face. But her eyes were red. *I'd made her cry?* Something about them looked irreparable. Final. *Just like what I'd done to Grandma and Grandpa.*

"Jayne?" My voice quivered.

129

"Ben—you shouldn't ever have blamed yourself for your grandparents' death."

My knee buckled at her unexpected words, and I fell against the doorframe, tottering a few inches from her face.

She drew back. "There's a reason they call it an *accident.* It wasn't anyone's fault."

It was like she could see into my soul and read me like a book. My voice cracked. "If I'd just gone to school in Albany, though, they wouldn't have made that trip that day. They wouldn't have been in the wrong place at the wrong time. They never wanted me to go to school in New Hampshire. It disappointed them."

Slowly, she shook her head. "I never met them, but I can't dream of a world where your loving grandma and grandpa could be disappointed in you."

But they were. They had been. I'd known that for eight years.

No, Ben. The voice whispered again, and this time I recognized it as Grandma's. *We're immensely proud of you. We love you and always will.*

I gripped the doorframe to keep myself upright. My mind swung like a huge pendulum.

Jayne gave me one last, red-eyed glance. "Good-bye, Ben. Good luck in New York." The door clicked shut with finality.

"Jayne?" I whispered, still reeling from her words—and from what seemed like Grandma's. Were they? Could they be true? My head throbbed. I pressed my palm against the wood. "Can't we talk about it?"

No response. I waited, begged silently, hoping she'd change her mind, open the door.

She didn't.

"I'm going." *I'll miss you.*

***

The drive to Albany was a blur. Once I got home, I took the boxes of Christmas cheer into Grandma and Grandpa's cheerless, deserted house.

I sat down on top of one of the plastic tubs and put my head in my hands.

Throughout all this effort, I'd been trying to *do* Christmas by recreating the ambience—lights and decorations and the delicious scent of the fresh pine tree. But the principal thing my grandparents had provided to make the season special was this: *love*.

They'd given me, the house, each other—love. Pure, unrestrained love.

Like Jayne had been giving to me with her nurturing, her affection, her everything. She'd given me back my grandparent's love.

For the first time in my life since they died, I'd experienced that gift once again. And within minutes I'd inadvertently thrown it away.

To find and then lose Jayne in such a short time—it was emotional whiplash. It felt like a whole NFL team of linemen had run me down. They'd need to carry me out on a stretcher. I lay on the floor, blood rushing in my ears, missing her, missing *me with her.*

I had to convince her to trust me again, that I wasn't just kissing and dissing her. That she could give *us* a try.

Then, in a flash—I knew what to do.

The perfect apology streaked across my night sky like a chorus of angels from on high.

Chapter 24

Jayne

On Christmas, I finished up all the leftovers in the fridge. Seneca genuinely was a great cook. That night, I dunked the last of the cookies in milk and ate those, too.

Was I overeating? Totally.

Binge-eating.

Comfort-eating.

Fog-eating.

Over the past two days, I'd watched all the guests' favorite Christmas movies—twice. I'd sat at the piano and plunked out my best "Jingle Bells," and sang along at the top of my lungs to drown out the silence. I'd opened the pair of Christmas pajamas I'd brought as a gift for Calder and worn them.

I'd opened and shut the music box a hundred thousand times—and resisted throwing it in the fire.

It was too pretty to throw in the fire.

But I did burn the wrapping paper it came in. That counted.

The tree was depressing to look out, now that Ben had removed all his grandmother's ornaments and the lights. *I didn't even get to look at it on Christmas Eve or Christmas.*

Then, Christmas ended. The clock inexorably ticked on to the last stroke of the doomed day. Finally, it was time to lug out the tree—not an easy task on my own, and needles got everywhere.

I cleaned the place, repacked my car, and headed toward Albany.

Goodbye, Wildwood Lodge.

So much for holiday togetherness. Apparently, I couldn't have Christmas Eve or Christmas Day with my family, or with friends, or even with strangers, as it turned out.

Maybe I should book one of those holiday cruises next year and just spend the whole two two-week holiday at the buffet table and listen to marginally talented lounge singers.

Back at home, I de-holidayed my SUV, and then tried to pull myself together to go back to work on the twenty-seventh.

Please say I won't have to attend an office New Year's Eve party. Please say that Ben will wisely stay far away from my cubicle and not acknowledge my existence. Please?

I'd already texted Gilda and warned her sternly that there should be zero mention of Ben Bellamy and his connection to my failed Christmas venture. Or to my failed holiday crush on him.

Perfect Christmas? Ha! Perfect disaster. From stem to stern.

Chapter 25

Jayne

The WGWG station buzzed with the usual energy, and at my cubicle, there were about fifty unopened product boxes from local businesses hoping to be featured on my show. I opened the first one. Ah, look. A toilet brush shaped like a Valentine heart—and in pink and red, my favorite color combination.

I flumped down in my chair. I couldn't even muster enthusiasm for tinsel hearts.

"Any texts from you-know-who?" Gilda asked.

"None to speak of."

"How about to not speak of?"

The woman could pry, but I'd never tell her that Ben had texted me a couple of times since I'd pushed him away a week ago, but that I couldn't bring myself to read them. Maybe in January, when the holidays were over. When he was truly gone from my life. Then it'd be nostalgic, charming to think back on the charmed Christmas week we'd spent together.

"It's time to film, girl. Put on a smile. Fake, if you have to."

I had to.

It was time to go live. I pasted on a smile, but anyone who knew me would've seen it was forced.

"Hey, guys. Happy New Year's Eve," I said to the camera, beaming. "Plain Jayne here. You're going to love what I've found for all of you today—since I've been doing exactly what you all have been doing the past two days—Christmas clearance shopping!" That statement was only true if all my viewers had also been wallowing in sorrow. "Let's get ready to rejoice in the discount deals!"

At least I could feign rejoicing in deals.

"Let's start with this cute Santa-faced doorknob cover with dangling bells. It's too soon to remove Santa from the house," I rambled on, faking it. The spot ended, and I'd managed to keep my mascara from smudging.

"Jayne?" Gilda breezed up and handed me a mug of steaming brew as I stepped out of the lights. We walked to my desk where I sat down with a heavy thud. "There's someone new on staff you should meet."

My head flopped backward and I stared up at Gilda. "Do I have to? I'm depleted. What if I can't shake hands or my fingers fall off when I do?"

"Hi." A tall redhead with straight hair and a straight nose and a straight figure and pencil skirt—the embodiment of verticality—greeted me. "I'm Alessandra."

Where had I heard that name? "You used to be on Marty and Marissa's show." I stood up to shake her hand. I was exhausted, but I could be polite.

"You watched it?"

No, but I'd heard. "What can you tell me about working with them?" I waited while Alessandra hemmed and hawed. "It's okay. I'm the soul of discretion. I actually ran into both of them over Christmas, and Marty mentioned the change of direction the show took recently. He mentioned you, too."

"He actually knew my name?" she scoffed and looked around the newsroom. "I've never been in such a hostile work environment in all

135

my life."

That was all I needed to know to help me make my decision.

A career move to Boston to work for Marty and Marissa was off the table. Fame was not worth it.

"Thanks for being open with me. I won't tell a soul." I wouldn't need to. I wasn't ever having anything to do with that brother-sister duo again.

"I'm just glad to be at WGWG. My parents are so happy I'm here."

Lucky Alessandra. One more level of so-called success to my resume was never going to convince Mom and Dad, or any of my siblings, that I was worth their notice. In fact, what I did for work in general probably already embarrassed them on some level.

"It's nice your family values what you do for a living." My parents and siblings didn't value the same things I did. "I grew up a Fancy Nancy in a Plain Jane family."

"Is that what inspired you to name your show? Tongue in cheek, of course."

"Probably so." Ha. Alessandra got me. "Mom and Dad are focused on making the world better by digging wells in third-world villages. My siblings have their own crusades. I just want to make people's worlds happier, one sparkly bauble at a time."

"All of us are doing life in our own way." Alessandra tapped her drink mug against mine. "There are a lot of ways to do life right."

"Good point." I'd never do life their way, and vice versa.

I can live with that. But I just wish they'd love me and include me sometimes.

That wasn't too much to ask, was it?

"Marty and Marissa didn't deserve you."

"No, they didn't." Alessandra left me at my cubicle.

When Alessandra left, I wasted no time. I shot an email telling them thanks, but no, thanks. It hurt a little to say goodbye to a dream, but sometimes a dream was wrong, and I needed to let it die.

136

A few days went by, and blessedly, I didn't run into Ben. Finally, the curiosity snagged me, and I sought out O'Keefe, Ben's producer.

"Ben went to New York City. Didn't you hear? I thought everyone had heard. One of our own—interviewing for the big market. Wow. But, hey. Don't be jealous! I know you're jealous. Okay, we all are. Ben's on his way up. Talent from here to the moon." O'Keefe slapped my back. "Sorry your thing with Marty and Marissa didn't work out, Jayne. We were all rooting for you."

"How did you hear about that?"

"Their producers called last month and asked for clips of your past shows. That kind of thing is never a secret." He guffawed and headed back to his cubicle.

I slunk to mine. So much for my secret foray into career advancement.

Now, everyone knew about my failure—or at least *they* likely thought of it as a failure. I knew better how to define it: an opportunity rejected, while waiting for something better to happen.

Because it would. I just knew it in my soul.

But, I miss Ben. Somehow my soul also knows Ben should be part of whatever great thing happens to me—or else it won't be great.

"Jayne, you all right?" Gilda brought me a cruller from the break room. Someone had been leveling up their baking skills over the holiday. "The staff New Year's Eve party starts in a few minutes. Did you bring a white elephant for the gift exchange?"

I grabbed my wrapped gift and trudged toward the conference room. Everyone wore party hats and gold masks, and they were letting loose to loud holiday music. Mistletoe hung over the center of the massive conference table, so it would take acrobatics to angle someone beneath it. Good call.

The staff was in full jollity mode. Normally, I would've been feeling festive, too. But not today.

Gilda grabbed my elbow and pulled me near the boom box that

played the last verse of "White Christmas," the song Ben and I had danced to. I stutter-stepped, my feet glued to the floor until it ended and I could move again.

A bad pop song played next, nothing holiday about it.

Good. I shook my groove thing for a few minutes with Gilda and Rita the lighting director.

"How was Wildwood Lodge?" Rita asked. "I heard you were there when Ben arrived. Were you kind of shocked? He's usually so no-nonsense when he's off-camera. Did he turn the lodge into an igloo with his icy stare? He's so stinking traditional. He would never be fun at a party you were throwing. You'd keep it fun—fresh. Wacky."

Wacky. That was me.

Traditional Christmases, holidays. With warmth and friendship. Calm skating on the pond. Sitting around the fire reading, or singing at the piano.

Those things felt a lot more *right* than this weird, manufactured festivity. This—to me—was the nightclub version of a holiday.

I wanted family.

I wanted home.

I wanted Ben and his version of the world.

My phone rang. I used it as an excuse to dash away from the mosh pit area of the staff party.

"Hello?" I answered without checking the caller. "Thank you for calling. Even if you're just asking to renew my car warranty, I bless you for it."

"Jayne?" Ben's unmistakable voice was on the other end of the line. "Hey. How are you?"

"Me?" Terrible. Because there was a lump in my throat the size of the Big Apple. "I heard you're in New York."

"Uh, I was."

And? "And you're not now?"

"There's someone here who wants to talk to you."

A million *someones'* faces scrolled through my brain. *Please don't*

138

let it be Marissa begging me to come onto her show to be the butt of all her and Marty's jokes.

"Okay," I eked out. "Who is it?"

But instead of answering, he must have handed off the phone, and a familiar female voice came on. "Jaynie? Jayne-the-Pain-in-the-Rain?"

My childhood nickname. "Joanie?" What in the–? "Why are you with Ben?" Ben was in New York City, not Saratoga Springs where Joanie lived. And Joanie didn't know Ben, and vice versa, and—

"Oh, my goodness, Jayne. You didn't tell me you knew Ben Bellamy!" She hooted as only Joanie could hoot. "Get your cute self over here! Ben insisted that you'd want to be invited. When he showed up at the door, though, I swear, I thought I was winning some kind of Publisher's Clearinghouse Sweepstakes. You know, since he's on the news and stuff?"

"Joanie, what's going on?"

"I mean, you're on TV, too, but he's Ben Bellamy, and—"

Blessedly, Ben came back on the line. "Your family said they'd like you to come to their holiday get-together. They never invite you because you're always busy on TV with your career and things. Yeah, I know, I know. The excuse was pretty lame on their part—no offense, Joanie—but they're apologetic, and they're sincere. Come over. Will you? Please?"

"Me?" There were still so many parts of this conversation that I wasn't following, but I didn't care. "I can be there in a half hour, if traffic allows."

"Well, come as fast as the winter roads allow. Otherwise, your mom is going to force-feed me some kind of poi recipe she discovered in Ethiopia. And you know how I am about *traditional* holiday food."

"I'll pick up a spiral-cut ham on my way."

"This is why I love you."

Love? Those four letters got me through traffic, through the drive-up grocery market, and to Joanie's in twenty-five minutes.

Ben met me at the door, the twenty-pound ham banging against my thigh. "Ben!" I breathed, but Joanie rushed forward and shouldered him out of the way.

"Jayne! I'm so glad you came." She hugged me, and then four of her six kids mobbed me.

"Aunt Jayne! Did you bring presents?"

"If you think ham is a present, then yes."

"Thank you!" They hugged the ham and took it inside. Maxie, the oldest, called over her shoulder. "You saved us from that Ethiopian food, Jayne. You're our hero!"

Joanie pulled us inside, where the whole Renwick family was together—quite the crowd—and we were absorbed, with no chance for a heart-to-heart.

Over the course of the afternoon and evening, we listened to Mom and Dad's latest adventures with humanitarian aid. They'd been in Africa digging wells for the past three months and only arrived home last night. Then, we played charades, sang at Joanie's piano while Maxie played at the edge of her abilities, and told stories.

My family had included me. They didn't even act like I was a stranger to them. Instead, they were as warm—and as oblivious of their earlier sidelining—toward me as I could ever wish.

In the kitchen, over her third plate of ham, Joanie hugged me. "I'm so glad you came! If we'd known you would say yes, we would have always invited you."

"You could have just checked. It's nice to be invited."

"But you said no for a long time, so we figured …"

"When did I say no? I mean, back when I was working my way up through the ranks in a retail store, getting my decorator's credentials, I might have."

"Yes, then, and after that when you got famous on TV, you were always complaining about your work schedule being so grueling—getting up at three a.m. We all know Renwicks are night owls. We didn't want to add to your stress."

True. I'd never considered that. "You didn't want to make me miserable."

"You're not very pleasant when you're tired. I remember when you were four years old, and ... Well, I guess you're not four anymore. Ha!" Joanie tapped my arm. "And we should all remember that. You're not a kid, even though I'll always think of you as my baby sister. Do you know, I prayed you here to Earth? I prayed for you every day. At Christmas, I begged Santa for a baby sister year after year, and then—Christmas morning when I was fourteen, Mom announced she was having you. We all shouted like we'd just been told we'd won the lottery."

Me. Wanted. Wished for. Prayed for.

Really?

"I ..." My voice caught. "No one ever told me that."

"Of course we did! Well, maybe not when you were old enough to remember it. I moved out when you were five. You had Mom and Dad all to yourself. Lucky."

"Well, I had to share them with the destitute nations of the world."

"Yeah. There's that." Joanie rolled her eyes. "They took you with them."

"Uh-huh."

"I always figured you loved that, but come to think of it, I bet you didn't love that. I bet you missed out on a normal childhood."

At that moment, Ben walked in. "And yet, she stands before you, a strong, independent woman who knows her tinsel."

"Ben hates tinsel," I said to Joanie in a stage whisper.

Joanie laughed, took another heaping plate of ham, and kissed my cheek. "I'm happy for you, Baby Sister. You've got a great man there."

I did? I did.

We were finally alone for the first time all evening. I took Ben to Joanie's husband's study, which had a nice, big Christmas tree beside bookshelves and a recliner.

"Okay, my friend. Explain what's going on here." I directed him to sit in the leather chair, while I stood, leaning against the arm of the sofa.

He did sit, but he leaned on the edge. "I found Joanie online, dropped by this afternoon, as soon as I arrived from the City, and she acted like I was some kind of celebrity. She agreed you needed an invitation. Your family is great, by the way. I'd totally misjudged them."

Me, too. "You misjudged them based on information from me."

"It's in the past now."

"Tell me about New York. About Marissa. About … you know." *Whether or not you love me. Which—it seems like you do.* I bit my lips together, holding a breath. This explanation would make or break me.

"What you saw that night. With Marissa. It was a misunderstanding—on Marissa's part most of all."

Oh. Wait, really? But on my part too, he implied.

"She threw herself at me when I told her that I'd made progress emotionally, and that I was ready to move forward in my career. She misinterpreted that statement as my being ready to come back *to her.* You walked in just at that moment—but she was wrong. I'd already told her I was seeing you. That it was new, but that I was serious about you." He reached for my hands.

Oh. All I could think was monosyllabic *ohs.* "Go on." I took his hands. He pulled me off my place on the couch's arm and toward him. Our knees knocked.

"I went to New York. I'd been putting it off for so long—waiting until I'd cleared things up in my life."

"Like what?"

"Like … something I should have told you earlier."

My kneecap trembled. "What's that?"

"It began when I applied to college. They'd been unhappy that I didn't attend school in Albany, but had gone to Dartmouth in New Hampshire instead—a long way from home. They'd seen it as a betrayal. Double that when I didn't choose sports reporting, Grandpa's dream career, as my own path." He winced. "I thought I could be more useful to the world through psychology. And then …"

"Ben." My heart was squeezing as if in a vise. I sat down, balancing on his knee. "I had no idea."

"I've never told anyone about this. About why I needed to finish up unfinished business."

This was painful for him, and I reached my arm around him, waiting until he could talk again. Soon, he did.

"The day of my master's degree hooding ceremony, I invited my grandparents to come and see me receive my diploma. Their car hit a deer on the drive home from the graduation. They didn't make it."

His voice was flat, stoic.

My heart lurched, and I buried my face in his shoulder. "Oh, Ben."

He placed a hand on the small of my back. "I was left with their house, and their memories, and their unfinished lives."

"And you needed to finish what was undone."

He nodded. "I took the sports reporter job, although I incorporated my own skills and interests into it. I maintained their house, their yard, their friendships. I even sang in their church choir."

"But, Ben." That lump in my throat was now the size of the Big Pineapple instead of just an apple. "They wouldn't have wanted you to do that."

"Maybe not, but I felt so culpable."

"And … Christmas was the final piece?"

With a heavy expulsion of breath, he said, "I needed to complete one last Christmas on their behalf. A *perfect* Christmas. Like Grandma Bonnie would have wanted." He looked up at me at last, his blue eyes the color of a clear mountain stream. "You gave that to me. The chance—and you helped me complete it. I owe you so much. And for that reason, I went to New York."

Non sequitur? "I'm sorry. I don't understand how it fits."

The clock on the bookshelf chimed midnight. A muffled cheer rose in the background.

"I'd told myself I wouldn't entertain the idea of leaving Albany until I'd completed that bucket list, and that I wouldn't take any interviews. But when I did, thanks to you, I had a few stipulations for taking the job."

"You were offered a job?" An actual offer! My balloon floated to the ceiling—then popped and fell on the floor in a latex heap. "So, you're leaving." I jumped to my feet.

Ben stood, too. "I told WNNN I'd work for them if I could bring along a talented colleague." He stepped close to me, moving my hands to his neck and placing his hands on my hips. "I meant you."

"Me? In New York? At WNNN?" My world careened like a car on black ice.

But then, Ben righted it—because his lips were on mine, and I went straight to my happy place, my safe space: Ben Bellamy's embrace. I stayed there, kissing him in Joanie's husband's study, while festive sounds of my family waxed and waned in the other room, until they all sang "Auld Lang Syne."

"Will you come with me? To New York?"

"And be your on-air sidekick?"

"And be a lot more than that, Jayne. It's moved really fast, but I'm taking my speed cues from Lester and Chieko. When it's right, it's right. I've met your family. They love me—clearly."

"As they should."

"How about you, Jayne? Can you love me? Just Benson Smith, not the TV persona Ben Bellamy? Enough to be plain Jayne Smith?"

"When I'm with you, nothing will ever be plain." I kissed him to show him just how not-plain life with me could be, too.

Epilogue

Jayne

"Next up, we have Ben and Jayne, WNNN's cutest young couple. Like every morning, they'll discuss the psychology of life and relationships with special guests. Today they'll be on with Marty and Marissa, who've flown in from Boston to meet their rivals for cutest couple on daytime television status. After the break."

That intro! I could hardly bear it. If whoever did the bumper spot's dialogue had had any idea about Ben's and my last in-person brush with Marty and Marissa, they would never have written something that would inflame the brother-sister team's feelings so flagrantly.

"Are you ready to be on camera?" Ben sidled up to me. Oh, he looked good in that bright blue suit. Hot video, for sure. "You look amazing, Jayne. That maternity dress is on point."

"It shows off your contribution to our family extremely well." I patted my rounding belly. "Are you okay with using this spot with your ex-girlfriend to announce what we're naming our baby girl? That's not awkward?"

"It's totally awkward—and our viewers will eat it for breakfast."

145

True. Ben did know the psychology of TV viewers, and I'd become a not-too-shabby expert on them myself over the past months since we'd gone on air as newlywed co-hosts. I'd read tons of articles and books, and though I didn't have the formal training of my hot husband, I could hold my own whether we interviewed a football coach or a famous chef. It was fun. And funny. And the audiences—as Ben said—ate us for breakfast. Or, with breakfast.

He kissed my forehead. "You look beautiful. As soon as this baby is here, let's make another one. And another. I want a whole passel of them to take skating at Wildwood Lodge."

"If you take lessons."

"I will, if you give them." He handed me an envelope. "Christmas gift. Early."

I opened it, confused. "It's a sheaf of legal documents?"

No time to examine them, and he took them back. "We'll look at these again soon."

We were shuffled into our barrel chairs onstage, and the hot lights were set for the camera. Onto the set came our two old friends, Marty and Marissa.

The conversational banter sparked to life as the camera rolled.

Marty started. "What viewers of 'Breakfast with Ben and Jayne' don't know is that we tried to hire Jayne just a month before she and Ben got engaged and started working in New York. That was right before their big wedding, which *you* all saw." He looked at the camera. "Event of the decade, they called it." He waited for the live audience to react.

Marissa jumped in. "And what else no one knew is that Ben and I had a little thing between us before he met Jayne." She reached over and patted Ben's knee. I colored and fake-swatted her hand away.

The audience roared, like this was both an off-limits move and an unbelievable story.

Ben took the volley. "Lucky for me, Jayne won my heart. And now, what you're all here for today—we're letting Marty and Marissa play Word Scramble Puzzle for you, our viewers, to guess the name of our baby. Baby Girl Bellamy will be born in just six weeks, and we're ready to reveal her name on live television."

The people in the audience ate it up. They loved Marty and Marissa, and they finally guessed the name we'd chosen: Albany Bellamy. They didn't need to know that her last name would legally be Smith.

Then, Marty took center stage, standing right in front of Ben and me.

"And the surprise Marissa and I have for you, Jayne, is we've had all your siblings brought to the studio today, here in New York, and we're hosting a live baby shower for you, on national television."

My jaw dropped. "My family? Is here?"

The audience ahhed, and we went to commercial break.

No way! I ran to the wings, where I met Mom and my sisters. My dad and brothers were gathered around the craft-services table, eating bagels and muffins.

Dad came over with a huge plate of grub. "Do you eat like this every day? I can't say I blame you for taking the TV job. The people we work with all over the world would be inspired."

Inspired? Not appalled? "Thanks, Dad." I hugged him, my pregnant belly getting in the way.

"I never knew your job was so intense," Mom said, her plate full as well. "Did you see all the people milling around and working to make this event look so professional? It's incredible. And you're the one they're all revolving around. Jayne, I had no idea." She hugged me next. "But I'm most proud of you and Ben and the family you're creating."

"Thanks, Mom." I hugged her, and then each of my sisters and sisters-in-law in succession. They were used to Ben by now, but they all went starry-eyed over Marty and Marissa when we introduced them.

"Commercial ends in thirty seconds." Our producer, Gilda, shuffled them toward their seats. "Are you ready to be onstage?"

"We get to be like you?" Joanie said, giddy. "I'm so excited. I've always wanted to be like you, Jayne." She kissed my cheek, probably leaving a lipstick smudge.

"Sorry, we've gotten bumped. Hold places for three minutes," said Gilda. The break extended due to breaking news. It was New York. Things happened. A lot.

Ben cornered me, while my family fawned over Marty and Marissa.

"Jayne, you did it." He handed me the legal papers again.

"Did what?" But I knew. He meant I'd made my life into something my family admired. Although, it turned out they might have admired it all along. "I couldn't have done any of it without you."

"Well, that's true." He kissed my neck—below the makeup line. "Not the Albany Bellamy Smith part, anyway. That took two of us. Now, will you check out my present to you?"

"It's a contract."

"Yeah. For me to teach classes at the community college near our townhouse."

"You're becoming a teacher?" I instantly pictured him in a button-up plaid shirt with a cardigan—the kind with patches on the sleeves. Heavy-rimmed glasses. His devastating good looks. He'd be every college girl's first-snowfall wish for love.

"See? Your snowfall wish came true. You finally got your hot teacher."

"Ben!" I lightly punched his arm for teasing me.

"Just giving my wife what she wants. Granting her every wish."

So, so many wishes came true because of Ben. "You'll be the hottest teacher on campus."

He nuzzled my ear. "The hottest teacher you ever made a baby with."

"For sure." I tilted my head back and let him kiss my neck.

"Places, everyone." Gilda clapped and we hustled back to work. Along with my family, we found our places. Together.

Snowfall Wishes Series

Wildwood Lodge

Seacliff Chateau

Maplebrook Bridge

Acknowledgments

Thanks go to Louise Tolman for allowing me a space to write when I had no place to go. Thank you for following that prompting to invite me.

And to Mary and Paula for valued editing advice.

Always, thanks to my beloved husband for being my alpha reader and the first in everything in my heart.

About the Author

Jennifer Griffith is the *USA Today* bestselling author of clean, escapist fiction she calls Cotton Candy for the Soul. She and her family live in the rural Arizona desert, where the winter is seldom snowy, but she loves Christmas and cocoa and all things cozy.

Made in United States
Orlando, FL
17 January 2022

13590305R00098